Thomas Nelson Page

Among the Camps

Young people's stories of the war

Thomas Nelson Page

Among the Camps
Young people's stories of the war

ISBN/EAN: 9783337425753

Printed in Europe, USA, Canada, Australia, Japan

Cover: Foto ©Andreas Hilbeck / pixelio.de

More available books at **www.hansebooks.com**

AMONG THE CAMPS

OR

YOUNG PEOPLE'S STORIES OF THE WAR

BY

THOMAS NELSON PAGE

ILLUSTRATED

NEW YORK

CHARLES SCRIBNER'S SONS

1891

Press of J. J. Little & Co.
Astor Place, New York

To Her:

NOTE.

My acknowledgments are due to Messrs. Harper & Brothers and to Mr. A. B. Starey, the Publishers and the Editor of HARPERS' YOUNG PEOPLE, in which Magazine I had the pleasure of having these stories, with the accompanying illustrations, first appear.

T. N. P.

CONTENTS.

LIST OF ILLUSTRATIONS.

A CAPTURED SANTA CLAUS.

I.

HOLLY HILL was the place for Christmas! From Bob down to brown-eyed Evelyn, with her golden hair floating all around her, every one hung up a stocking, and the visit of Santa Claus was the event of the year.

They went to sleep on the night before Christmas—or rather they went to bed, for sleep was long far from their eyes, —with little squeakings and gurglings, like so many little white mice, and if Santa Claus had not always been so very punctual in disappearing up the chimney before daybreak, he must certainly have been caught ; for by the time the chickens were crowing in the morning there would be an answering twitter through the house, and with a patter of little feet and subdued laughter small white-clad figures would steal through the dim light of dusky rooms and passages, opening doors with sudden bursts, and shouting "Christmas gift!" into darkened chambers, at still sleeping elders, then scurrying away in the gray light to rake open the hickory embers and revel in the exploration of their crowded stockings.

Such was Christmas morning at Holly Hill in the old times before the war. Thus it was, that at Christmas 1863, when there were no new toys to be had for love or money, there were much disappointment and some murmurs at Holly Hill. The children had never really felt the war until then, though their father, Major Stafford, had been off, first with his company and then with his regiment, since April, 1861. Now from Mrs. Stafford down to little tot Evelyn, there was an absence of the merriment which Christmas always brought with it. Their mother had done all she could to collect such presents as were within her reach, but the youngsters were much too sharp not to know that the presents were "just fixed up"; and when they were all gathered around the fire in their mother's chamber, Christmas morning, looking over their presents, their little faces wore an expression of pathetic disappointment.

"I don't think much of *this* Christmas," announced Ran, with characteristic gravity, looking down on his presents with an air of contempt. "A hatchet, a ball of string, and a hare-trap isn't much."

Mrs. Stafford smiled, but the smile soon died away into an expression of sadness.

"I too have to do without my Christmas gift," she said. "Your father wrote me that he hoped to spend Christmas with us, and he has not come."

"Never mind; he may come yet," said Bob encouragingly. (Bob always was encouraging. That was why he was

"Old Bob.") "An axe was just the thing I wanted, mamma," said he, shouldering his new possession proudly.

Mrs. Stafford's face lit up again.

"And a hatchet was what I wanted," admitted Ran; "now I can make my own hare-traps."

"An' I like a broked knife," asserted Charlie stoutly, falling valiantly into the general movement, whilst Evelyn pushed her long hair out of her eyes, and hugged her baby, declaring:

"I love my dolly, and I love Santa Tlaus, an' I love my papa," at which her mother took the little midget to her bosom, doll and all, and hid her face in her tangled curls.

II.

THE holiday was scarcely over when one evening Major Stafford galloped up to the gate, his black horse Ajax splashed with mud to his ear-tips.

The Major soon heard all about the little ones' disappointment at not receiving any new presents.

"Santa Tlaus didn' tum this Trismas, but he's tummin' next Trismas," said Evelyn, looking wisely up at him, that evening, from the rug where she was vainly trying to make her doll's head stick on her broken shoulders.

"And why did he not come this Christmas, Miss Wisdom?" laughed her father, touching her with the toe of his boot.

"Tause the Yankees wouldn' let him," said she gravely, holding her doll up and looking at it pensively, her head on one side.

"And why, then, should he come next year?"

"Tause God's goin' to make him." She turned the mutilated baby around and examined it gravely, with her shining head set on the other side.

"There's faith for you," said Mrs. Stafford, as her husband asked, "How do you know this?"

"Tause God told me," answered Evelyn, still busy with her inspection.

" He did ? What is Santa Claus going to bring you ?"

The little mite sprang to her feet. " He's goin' to bring me—a—great—big—dolly—with real sure 'nough hair, and blue eyes that will go to sleep." Her face was aglow, and she stretched her hands wide apart to give the size.

"She has dreamt it," said the Major, in an undertone, to her mother. " There is not such a doll as that in the Southern Confederacy," he continued.

The child caught his meaning. " Yes, he is," she insisted, " 'cause I asked him an' he said he would ; and Charlie——"

Just then that youngster himself burst into the room, a small whirlwind in petticoats. As soon as his cyclonic tendencies could be curbed, his father asked him :

"Well, what did you ask Santa Claus for, young man ?"

" For a pair of breeches and a sword," answered the boy, promptly, striking an attitude.

"Well, upon my word !" laughed his father, eying the erect little figure and the steady, clear eyes which looked proudly up at him. " I had no idea what a young Achilles we had here. You shall have them."

The boy nodded gravely. " All right. When I get to be a man I won't let anybody make my mamma cry." He advanced a step, with head up, the very picture of spirit.

"Ah ! you won't ?" said his father, with a gesture to prevent his wife interrupting.

" Nor my little sister," said the young warrior, patron-
izingly, swelling with infantile importance.

" No ; he won't let anybody make *me* ky," chimed in
Evelyn, promptly accepting the proffered protection.

" On my word, Ellen, the fellow has some of the old blood
in him," said Major Stafford, much pleased. " Come here,
my young knight." He drew the boy up to him. " I had
rather have heard you say that than have won a brigadier's
wreath. You shall have your breeches and your sword next
Christmas. Were I the king I should give you your spurs.
Remember, never let any one make your mother or sister
cry."

Charlie nodded in token of his acceptance of the condition.

"All right," he said.

III.

WHEN Major Stafford galloped away, on his return
to his command, the little group at the lawn gate
shouted many messages after him. The last thing he
heard was Charlie's treble, as he seated himself on the gate-
post, calling to him not to forget to make Santa Claus bring
him a pair of breeches and a sword, and Evelyn's little voice
reminding him of her " dolly that can go to sleep."

Many times during the ensuing year, amid the hardships
of the campaign, the privations of the march, and the dangers
of battle, the Major heard those little voices calling to him.
In the autumn he won the three stars of a colonel for gal-
lantry in leading a desperate charge on a town, in a perilous
raid into the heart of the enemy's country, and holding the
place ; but none knew, when he dashed into the town at the
head of his regiment under a hail of bullets, that his mind
was full of toyshops and clothing stores, and that when he
was so stoutly holding his position he was guarding a little
boy's suit, a small sword with a gilded scabbard, and a large
doll with flowing ringlets and eyes that could " go to sleep."
Some of his friends during that year had charged the Major
with growing miserly, and rallied him upon hoarding up his

pay and carrying large rolls of Confederate money about his person ; and when, just before the raid, he invested his entire year's pay in four or five ten-dollar gold pieces, they vowed he was mad.

The Major, however, always met these charges with a smile.   And as soon as his position was assured in the captured town he proved his sanity.

The owner of a handsome store on the principal street, over which was a large sign, " Men's and Boys' Clothes," peeping out, saw a Confederate major ride up to the door, which had been hastily fastened when the fight began, and rap on it with the handle of his sword.   There was something in the rap that was imperative, and fearing violence if he failed to respond, he hastily opened the door.   The officer entered, and quickly selected a little uniform suit of blue cloth with brass buttons.

" What is the price of this ? "

" Ten dollars," stammered the shopkeeper.

To his astonishment the Confederate officer put his hand in his pocket and laid a ten-dollar gold piece on the counter.

" Now show me where there is a toyshop."

There was one only a few doors off, and there the Major selected a child's sword handsomely ornamented, and the most beautiful doll, over whose eyes stole the whitest of rose-leaf eyelids, and which could talk and do other wonderful things.   He astonished this shopkeeper also by laying down another gold piece.   This left him but two or three more of

the proceeds of his year's pay, and these he soon handed over
a counter to a jeweller, who gave him a small package in
exchange.

All during the remainder of the campaign Colonel Stafford
carried a package carefully sealed, and strapped on behind
his saddle. His care of it and his secrecy about it were
the subjects of many jests among his friends in the brigade,
and when in an engagement his horse was shot, and the Colonel, under a hot fire, stopped and calmly unbuckled his bundle, and during the rest of the fight carried it in his hand,
there was a clamor that he should disclose the contents.
Even an offer to sing them a song would not appease them.

The brigade officers were gathered around a camp-fire that
night on the edge of the bloody field. A Federal officer,
Colonel Denby, who had been slightly wounded and captured
in the fight, and who now sat somewhat grim and moody
before the fire, was their guest.

"Now, Stafford, open the bundle and let us into the
secret," they all said. The Colonel, without a word, rose and
brought the parcel up to the fire. Kneeling down, he took
out his knife and carefully ripped open the outer cover.
Many a jest was levelled at him across the blazing logs as he
did so.

One said the Colonel had turned peddler, and was trying
to eke out a living by running the blockade on Lilliputian
principles ; another wagered that he had it full of Confederate bills ; a third, that it was a talisman against bullets, and

so on. Within the outer covering were several others ; but
at length the last was reached. As the Colonel ripped carefully, the group gathered around and bent breathlessly over
him, the light from the blazing camp-fire shining ruddily on
their eager, weather-tanned faces. When the Colonel put in
his hand and drew out a toy sword, there was a general ex-
clamation, followed by a dead silence ; but when he took the
doll from her soft wrapping, and then unrolled and held up
a pair of little trousers not much longer than a man's hand,
and just the size for a five-year-old boy, the men turned away
their faces from the fire, and more than one who had boys of
his own at home, put his hand up to his eyes.

One of them, a bronzed and weather-beaten officer, who
had charged the Colonel with being a miser, stretched himself out on the ground, flat on his face, and sobbed aloud as
Colonel Stafford gently told his story of Charlie and Evelyn.
Even the grim face of Colonel Denby looked somewhat
changed in the light of the fire, and he reached over for the
doll and gazed at it steadily for some time.

COLONEL STAFFORD OPENS THE BUNDLE.

IV.

DURING the whole year the children had been looking forward to the coming of Christmas. Charlie's outbursts of petulance and not rare fits of anger were invariably checked if any mention was made of his father's injunction, and at length he became accustomed to curb himself by the recollection of the charge he had received. If he fell and hurt himself in his constant attempt to climb up impossible places, he would simply rub himself and say, proudly, " I don't cry now, I am a knight, and next Christmas I am going to be a man, 'cause my papa's goin' to tell Santa Claus to bring me a pair of breeches and a sword." Evelyn could not help crying when she was hurt, for she was only a little girl; but she added to her prayer of " God bless and keep my papa, and bring him safe home," the petition, " Please, God, bless and keep Santa Tlaus, and let him come here Trismas."

Old Bob and Ran too, as well as the younger ones, looked forward eagerly to Christmas.

But some time before Christmas the steady advance of the Union armies brought Holly Hill and the Holly Hill children far within the Federal lines, and shut out all chance of their being reached by any message or thing from their father. The only Confederates the children ever saw now were the prisoners who were being passed back on their way to prison. The only news they ever received were the rumors which reached them from Federal sources. Mrs. Stafford's heart was heavy within her, and when, a day or two before Christmas, she heard Charlie and Evelyn, as they sat before the fire, gravely talking to each other of the long-expected presents which their father had promised that Santa Claus should bring them, she could stand it no longer. She took Bob and Ran into her room, and there told them that now it was impossible for their father to come, and that they must help her entertain " the children " and console them for their disappointment. The two boys responded heartily, as true boys always will when thrown on their manliness.

For the next two days Mrs. Stafford and both the boys were busy. Mrs. Stafford, when Charlie was not present, gave her time to cutting out and making a little gray uniform suit from an old coat which her husband had worn when he first entered the army; whilst the boys employed themselves, Bob in making a pretty little sword and scabbard out of an old piece of gutter, and Ran, who had a wonderful turn, in carving a doll from a piece of hard seasoned wood.

The day before Christmas they lost a little time in following and pitying a small lot of prisoners who passed along the road by the gate. The boys were always pitying the prisoners and planning means to rescue them, for they had an idea that they suffered a terrible fate. Only one certain case had come to their knowledge. A young man had one day been carried by the Holly Hill gate on his way to the head-quarters of the officer in command of that portion of the lines, General Denby. He was in citizen's clothes and was charged with being a spy. The next morning Ran, who had risen early to visit his hare-traps, rushed into his mother's room white-faced and wide-eyed.

"Oh, mamma!" he gasped, "they have hung him, just because he had on those clothes!"

Mrs. Stafford, though she was much moved herself, endeavored to explain to the boy that this was one of the laws of war; but Ran's mind was not able to comprehend the principles which imposed so cruel a sentence for what he deemed so harmless a fault.

This act and some other measures of severity gave General Denby a reputation of much harshness among the few old residents who yet remained at their homes in the lines, and the children used to gaze at him furtively as he would ride by, grim and stern, followed by his staff. Yet there were those who said that General Denby's rigor was simply the result of a high standard of duty, and that at bottom he had a soft heart.

V.

THE approach of Christmas was recognized even in the Federal camps, and many a song and ringing laugh were heard around the camp-fires, and in the tents and little cabins used as winter quarters, over the boxes which were pouring in from home. The troops in the camps near General Denby's headquarters on Christmas eve had been larking and frolicking all day like so many children, preparing for the festivities of the evening, when they proposed to have a Christmas tree and other entertainments; and the General, as he sat in the front room in the house used as his headquarters, writing official papers, had more than once during the afternoon frowned at the noise outside which had disturbed him. At length, however, late in the afternoon, he finished his work, and having dismissed his adjutant, he locked the door, and pushing aside all his business papers, took from his pocket a little letter and began to read.

As he read, the stern lines of the grim soldier's face relaxed, and more than once a smile stole into his eyes and stirred the corners of his grizzled moustache.

The letter was scrawled in a large childish hand. It ran :

"My Dearest Grandpapa : I want to see you very much. I send you a Christmas gift. I made it myself. I hope to get a whole lot of dolls and other presents. I love you. I send you all these kisses . .

. . . . . . You must kiss them.

"Your loving little granddaughter,

"Lily."

When he had finished reading the letter the old veteran gravely lifted it to his lips and pressed a kiss on each of the little spaces so carefully drawn by the childish hand.

When he had done he took out his handkerchief and blew his nose violently as he walked up and down the room. He even muttered something about the fire smoking. Then he sat down once more at his table, and placing the little letter before him, began to write. As he wrote, the fire smoked more than ever, and the sounds of revelry outside reached him in a perfect uproar; but he no longer frowned, and when the strains of " Dixie " came in at the window, sung in a clear, rich, mellow solo, he sat back in his chair and listened :

" I wish I were in Dixie, away, away ;
In Dixie's land I'll take my stand,
To live and die for Dixie land,
Away, away, away down South in Dixie ! "

sang the beautiful voice, full and sonorous.

When the song ended, there was an outburst of applause, and shouts apparently demanding some other song, which was refused, for the noise grew to a tumult. The General rose

and walked to the window. Suddenly the uproar hushed,
for the voice began again, but this time it was a hymn :

> " While shepherds watched their flocks by night,
>   All seated on the ground,
>   The angel of the Lord came down,
>   And glory shone around."

Verse after verse was sung, the men pouring out of their
tents and huts to listen to the music.

> "All glory be to God on high,
>   And to the earth be peace ;
>   Good will henceforth from Heaven to men
>   Begin and never cease ! "

sang the singer to the end. When the strain died away
there was dead silence.

The General finished his letter and sealed it. Carefully
folding up the little one which lay before him, he replaced it
in his pocket, and going to the door, summoned the orderly
who was just without.

"Mail that at once," he said.

" Yes, sir."

" By the way," as the soldier turned to leave, " who was
that singing out there just now ? I mean that last one, who
sang ' Dixie,' and the hymn."

" Only a peddler, sir, I believe."

The General's eyes fixed themselves on the soldier.

"Where did he come from ?"

"I don't know, sir. Some of the boys had him singing."

"Tell Major Dayle to come here immediately," said the General, frowning.

In a moment the officer summoned entered.

He appeared somewhat embarrassed.

"Who was this peddler?" asked the commander, sternly.

"I—I don't know—" began the other.

"You don't know! Where did he come from?"

"From Colonel Watchly's camp directly," said he, relieved to shift a part of the responsibility.

"How was he dressed?"

"In citizen's clothes."

"What did he have?"

"A few toys and trinkets."

"What was his name?"

"I did not hear it."

"And you let him go!" The General stamped his foot.

"Yes, sir; I don't think—" he began.

"No, I know you don't," said the General. "He was a spy. Where has he gone?"

"I—I don't know. He cannot have gone far."

"Report yourself under arrest," said the commander, sternly.

Walking to the door, he said to the sentinel:

"Call the corporal, and tell him to request Captain Albert to come here immediately."

In a few hours the party sent out reported that they had

traced the spy to a place just over the creek, where he was believed to be harbored.

"Take a detail and arrest him, or burn the house," ordered the General, angrily. "It is a perfect nest of treason," he said to himself as he walked up and down, as though in justification of his savage order.

"Or wait," he called to the captain, who was just withdrawing. "I will go there myself, and take it for my headquarters. It is a better place than this. I cannot stand this smoke any longer. That will break up their treasonable work."

VI.

ALL that day the tongues of the little ones at Holly Hill had been chattering unceasingly of the expected visit of Santa Claus that night. Mrs. Stafford had tried to explain to Charlie and Evelyn that it would be impossible for him to bring them their presents this year; but she was met with the undeniable and unanswerable statement that their father had promised them. Before going to bed they had hung their stockings on the mantelpiece right in front of the chimney, so that Santa Claus would be sure to see them.

The mother had broken down over Evelyn's prayer, "not to forget my papa, and not to forget my dolly," and her tears fell silently after the little ones were asleep, as she put the finishing touches to the tiny gray uniform for Charlie. She was thinking not only of the children's disappointment, but of the absence of him on whose promise they had so securely relied. He had been away now for a year, and she had had no word of him for many weeks. Where was he? Was he dead or alive? Mrs. Stafford sank on her knees by the bedside.

"O God, give me faith like this little child!" she prayed again and again. She was startled by hearing a step on the front portico and a knock at the door. Bob, who was work-

ing in front of the hall fire, went to the door. His mother
heard him answer doubtfully some question. She opened
the door and went out. A stranger with a large bundle or
pack stood on the threshold. His hat, which was still on
his head, was pulled down over his eyes, and he wore a
beard.

"An', leddy,' wad ye bay so koind as to shelter a poor
sthranger for a noight at this blissid toim of pace and good-
will?" he said, in a strong Irish brogue.

"Certainly," said Mrs. Stafford with her eyes fixed on
him. She moved slowly up to him. Then, by an instinct,
quickly lifting her hand, she pushed his hat back from his
eyes. Her husband clasped her in his arms.

"My darling!"

When the pack was opened, such a treasure-house of toys
and things was displayed as surely never greeted any other
eyes. The smaller children, including Ran, were not awaked,
at their father's request, though Mrs. Stafford wished to wake
them to see him; but Bob was let into the secrets, except
that he was not permitted to see a small package which
bore his name. Mrs. Stafford and the Colonel were like two
children themselves as they "tipped" about stuffing the long
stockings with candy and toys of all kinds. The beautiful
doll with flaxen hair, all arrayed in silk and lace, was seated,
last of all, securely on top of Evelyn's stocking, with her wardrobe just below her, where she would greet her young mistress
when she should first open her eyes, and Charlie's little blue

uniform was pinned beside the gray one his mother had made, with his sword buckled around the waist.

Bob was at last dismissed to his room, and the Colonel and Mrs. Stafford settled themselves before the fire, hand in hand, to talk over all the past. They had hardly started, when Bob rushed down the stairs and dashed into their room.

"Papa! papa! the yard's full of Yankees!"

Both the Colonel and Mrs. Stafford sprang to their feet.

"Through the back door!" cried Mrs. Stafford, seizing her husband.

"He cannot get out that way—they are everywhere; I saw them from my window," gasped Bob, just as the sound of trampling without became audible.

"Oh! what will you do? Those clothes! If they catch you in those clothes!" began Mrs. Stafford, and then stopped, her face growing ashy pale. Bob also turned even whiter than he had been before. He remembered the young man who was found in citizen's clothes in the autumn, and knew his dreadful fate. He burst out crying. "Oh, papa! will they hang you?" he sobbed.

"I hope not, my son," said the Colonel, gravely. "Certainly not, if I can prevent it." A gleam of amusement stole into his eyes. "It's an awkward fix, certainly," he added.

"You must conceal yourself," cried Mrs. Stafford, as a number of footsteps sounded on the porch, and a thundering knock shook the door. "Come here." She pulled him almost by main force into a closet or entry, and locked the door, just as the knocking was renewed. As the door was apparently about to be broken down, she went out into the hall. Her face was deadly white, and her lips were moving in prayer.

"Who's there?" she called, tremblingly, trying to gain time.

"Open the door immediately, or it will be broken down," replied a stern voice.

She turned the great iron key in the heavy old brass lock, and a dozen men rushed into the hall. They all waited for one, a tall elderly man in a general's fatigue uniform, and with a stern face and a grizzled beard. He addressed her.

"Madam, I have come to take possession of this house as my headquarters."

Mrs. Stafford bowed, unable to speak. She was sensible of a feeling of relief; there was a gleam of hope. If they did not know of her husband's presence   But the next word destroyed it.

"We have not interfered with you up to the present time, but you have been harboring a spy here, and he is here now."

"There is no spy here, and has never been," said Mrs. Stafford, with dignity; "but if there were, you should not know it from me." She spoke with much spirit. "It is not the custom of our people to deliver up those who have sought their protection."

The officer removed his hat. His keen eye was fixed on her white face. "We shall search the premises," he said sternly, but more respectfully than he had yet spoken. "Major, have the house thoroughly searched."

The men went striding off, opening doors and looking through the rooms. The General took a turn up and down the hall. He walked up to a door.

"That is my chamber," said Mrs. Stafford, quickly.

The officer fell back. "It must be searched," he said.

"My little children are asleep in there," said Mrs. Stafford, her face quite white.

"It must be searched," repeated the General. "Either they must do it, or I. You can take your choice."

Mrs. Stafford made a gesture of assent. He opened the door and stepped across the threshold. There he stopped. His eye took in the scene. Charlie was lying in the little trundle-bed in the corner, calm and peaceful, and by his side was Evelyn, her little face looking like a flower lying in the tangle of golden hair which fell over her pillow. The noise disturbed her slightly, for she smiled suddenly, and muttered something about "Santa Tlaus" and a "dolly." The officer's gaze swept the room, and fell on the overcrowded stockings hanging from the mantel. He advanced to the fireplace and examined the doll and trousers closely. With a curious expression on his face, he turned and walked out of the room, closing the door softly behind him.

"Major," he said to the officer in charge of the searching

party, who descended the steps just then, " take the men back
to camp, except the sentinels. There is no spy here." In a
moment Mrs. Stafford came out of her chamber. The old
officer was walking up and down in deep thought. Suddenly
he turned to her : " Madam, be so kind as to go and tell Colonel Stafford that General Denby desires him to surrender
himself." Mrs. Stafford was struck dumb. She was unable
to move or to articulate. " I shall wait for him," said the
General, quietly, throwing himself into an arm-chair, and
looking steadily into the fire.

VII.

A S his father concealed himself, Bob had left the chamber. He was in a perfect agony of mind. He knew that his father could not escape, and if he were found dressed in citizen's clothes he felt that he could have but one fate. All sorts of schemes entered his boy's head to save him. Suddenly he thought of the small group of prisoners he had seen pass by about dark. He would save him! Putting on his hat, he opened the front door and walked out. A sentinel accosted him surlily to know where he was going. Bob invited him in to get warm, and soon had him engaged in conversation.

"What do you do with your prisoners when you catch them?" inquired Bob.

"Send some on to prison—and hang some."

"I mean when you first catch them."

"Oh, they stay in camp. We don't treat 'em bad, without they be spies. There's a batch at camp now, got in this evening—sort o' Christmas gift." The soldier laughed as he stamped his feet to keep warm.

"Where's your camp?" Bob asked.

"About a mile from here, right on the road, or rather right on the hill at the edge of the pines 'yond the crick."

The boy left his companion, and sauntered in and out among the other men in the yard. Presently he moved on to the edge of the lawn beyond them. No one took further notice of him. In a second he had slipped through the gate, and was flying across the field. He knew every foot of ground as well as a hare, for he had been hunting and setting traps over it since he was as big as little Charlie. He had to make a detour at the creek to avoid the picket, and the dense briers were very bad and painful. However, he worked his way through, though his face was severely scratched. Into the creek he plunged. "Outch!" He had stepped into a hole, and the water was as cold as ice. However, he was through, and at the top of the hill he could see the glow of the camp fires lighting up the sky.

He crept cautiously up, and saw the dark forms of the sentinels pacing backward and forward wrapped in their over-coats, now lit up by the fire, then growing black against its blazing embers, then lit up again, and passing away into the shadow. How could he ever get by them? His heart began to beat and his teeth to chatter, but he walked boldly up.

"Halt! who goes there?" cried the sentry, bringing his gun down and advancing on him.

Bob kept on, and the sentinel, finding that it was only a boy, looked rather sheepish.

"Don't let him capture you, Jim," called one of them; "Call the Corporal of the Guard," another; "Order up the

reserves," a third ; and so on. Bob had to undergo something of an examination.

" I know the little Johnny," said one of them.

They made him draw up to the fire, and made quite a fuss
over him. Bob had his wits about him and soon learned that
a batch of prisoners were at a fire a hundred yards further
back. He therefore worked his way over there, although he
was advised to stay where he was and get dry, and had many
offers of a bunk from his new friends, some of whom followed
him over to where the prisoners were.

Most of them were quartered for the night in a hut before
which a guard was stationed. One or two, however, sat
around the camp-fire, chatting with their guards. Among
them was a major in full uniform. Bob singled him out ; he
was just about his father's size.

He was instantly the centre of attraction. Again he told
them he was from Holly Hill ; again he was recognized by
one of the men.

" Run away to join the army ?" asked one.

" No," said Bob, his eyes flashing at the suggestion.

" Lost ? "

" No."

" Mother whipped you ?"

" No."

As soon as their curiosity had somewhat subsided, Bob,
who had hardly been able to contain himself, said to the
Confederate major in a low undertone :

" My father, Colonel Stafford, is at home, concealed, and
the Yankees have taken possession of the house."

" Well ? " said the major, looking down at him as if
casually.

" He cannot escape, and he has on citizen's clothes,
and—" Bob's voice choked suddenly as he gazed at the
major's uniform.

" Well ? " The prisoner for a second looked sharply down
at the boy's earnest face. Then he put his hand under his
chin, and lifting it, looked into his eyes. Bob shivered and
a sob escaped him.

The major placed his hand firmly on his knee. " Why,
you are wringing wet," he said, aloud. " I wonder you are
not frozen to death." He rose and stripped off his coat.
" Here, get into this ; " and before the boy knew it the major
had bundled him into his coat, and rolled up the sleeves so
that Bob could use his hands. The action attracted the
attention of the rest of the group, and several of the Yankees
offered to take the boy and give him dry clothes.

" No, sir," laughed the major ; " this boy is a rebel. Do
you think he will wear one of your Yankee suits ? He's a
little major, and I'm going to give him a major's uniform."

In a minute he had stripped off his trousers, and was
helping Bob into them, standing himself in his underclothes
in the icy air. The legs were three times too long for the
boy, and the waist came up to his armpits.

" Now go home to your mother," said the major, laughing

at his appearance; "and some of you fellows get me some clothes or a blanket. I'll wear your Yankee uniform out of sheer necessity."

Bob trotted around, keeping as far away from the light of the camp-fires as possible. He soon found himself unobserved, and reached the shadow of a line of huts, and keeping well in it, he came to the edge of the camp. He watched his opportunity, and when the sentry's back was turned slipped out into the darkness. In an instant he was flying down the hill. The heavy clothes impeded him, and he stopped only long enough to snatch them off and roll them into a bundle, and sped on his way again. He struck the main road, and was running down the hill as fast as his legs could carry him, when he suddenly found himself almost on a group of dark objects who were standing in the road just in front of him. One of them moved. It was the picket. Bob suddenly stopped. His heart was in his throat.

"Who goes there?" said a stern voice. Bob's heart beat as if it would spring out of his body.

"Come in; we have you," said the man, advancing.

Bob sprang across the ditch beside the road, and putting his hand on the top rail of the fence, flung himself over it, bundle and all, flat on the other side, just as a blaze of light burst from the picket, and the report of a carbine startled the silent night. The bullet grazed the boy's arm, and crashed through the rail. In a second Bob was on his feet. The picket was almost on him. Seizing his bundle, he dived into the thicket as a half-dozen shots were sent ringing after him, the bullets hissing and whistling over his head. Several men dashed into the woods after him in hot pursuit, and a couple more galloped up the road to intercept him; but Bob's feet were winged, and he slipped through briers and brush like a scared hare. They scratched his face and threw him down, but he was up again. Now and then a shot crashed behind him, but he did not care for that; he thought only of being caught.

A few hundred yards up, he plunged into the stream, and wading across, was soon safe from his pursuers. Breathless, he climbed the hill, made his way through the woods, and emerged into the open fields. Across these he sped like a deer. He had almost given out. What if they should have caught his father, and he should be too late! A sob escaped him at the bare thought, and he broke again into a run, wiping off with his sleeve the tears that would come. The wind cut him like a knife, but he did not mind that.

As he neared the house he feared that he might be intercepted again and the clothes taken from him, so he stopped for a moment, and slipped them on once more, rolling up the sleeves and legs as well as he could. He crossed the yard undisturbed. He went around to the same door by which he had come out, for he thought this his best chance. The same sentinel was there, walking up and down, blowing his cold hands. Had his father been arrested? Bob's teeth chattered, but it was with suppressed excitement.

" Pretty cold," said the sentry.

" Ye—es," gasped Bob.

" Your mother's been out here, looking for you, I guess," said the soldier, with much friendliness.

" I rec—reckon so," panted Bob, moving toward the door. Did that mean that his father was caught ? He opened the door, and slipped quietly into the corridor.

General Denby still sat silent before the hall fire. Bob listened at the chamber door. His mother was weeping ; his father stood calm and resolute before the fire. He had determined to give himself up.

" If you only did not have on those clothes !" sobbed Mrs. Stafford. " If I only had not cut up the old uniform for the children !"

" Mother ! mother ! I have one !" gasped Bob, bursting into the room and tearing off the unknown major's uniform.

3

VIII.

TEN minutes later Colonel Stafford, with a steady step and a proud carriage, and with his hand resting on Bob's shoulder, walked out into the hall. He was dressed in the uniform of a Confederate major, which fitted admirably his tall, erect figure.

"General Denby, I believe," he said, as the Union officer rose and faced him. "We have met before under somewhat different circumstances," he said, with a bow, "for I now find myself your prisoner."

"I have the honor to request your parole," said the General, with great politeness, "and to express the hope that I may be able in some way to return the courtesy which I formerly received at your hands." He extended his hand and Colonel Stafford took it.

"You have my parole," said he.

"I was not aware," said the General, with a bow toward Mrs. Stafford, "until I entered the room where your children were sleeping, that I had the honor of your husband's acquaintance. I will now take my leave and return to camp, that I may not by my presence interfere with the joy of this season."

"I desire to introduce to you my son," said Colonel Stafford, proudly presenting Bob. "He is a hero."

The General bowed as he shook hands with him. Perhaps he had some suspicion how true a hero he was, for he rested his hand kindly on the boy's head, but he said nothing.

Both Colonel and Mrs. Stafford invited the old soldier to spend the night there, but he declined. He, however, accepted an invitation to dine with them next day.

Before leaving, he requested permission to take one more look at the sleeping children. Over Evelyn he bent silently. Suddenly stooping, he kissed her little pink cheek, and with a scarcely audible "Good-night," passed out of the room and left the house.

The next morning, by light, there was great rejoicing. Charlie and Evelyn were up betimes, and were laughing and chattering over their presents like two little magpies.

"Here's my sword and here's my breeches," cried Charlie, "two pair; but I'm goin' to put on my gray ones. I ain't goin' to wear a blue uniform."

"Here's my dolly!" screamed Evelyn, in an ecstasy over her beautiful present. And presently Bob and Ran burst in, their eyes fairly dancing.

"Christmas gift! It's a real one—real gold!" cried Bob, holding up a small gold watch, whilst Ran was shouting over a silver one of the same size.

That evening, after dinner, General Denby was sitting by

the fire in the Holly Hill parlor, with Evelyn nestled in his lap, her dolly clasped close to her bosom, and in the absence of Colonel Stafford, told Mrs. Stafford the story of the opening of the package by the camp-fire. The tears welled up into Mrs. Stafford's eyes and ran down her cheeks.

Charlie suddenly entered, in all the majesty of his new breeches, and sword buckled on hip. He saw his mother's tears. His little face flushed. In a second his sword was out, and he struck a hostile attitude.

"You sha'n't make my mamma cry !" he shouted.

"Charlie ! Charlie !" cried Mrs. Stafford, hastening to stop him.

"My papa said I was not to let any one make you cry," insisted the boy, stepping before his mother, and still keeping his angry eyes on the General.

"Oh, Charlie !" Mrs. Stafford took hold of him. "I am ashamed of you !—to be so rude !"

"Let him alone, madam," said the General. "It is not rudeness ; it is spirit—the spirit of our race. He has the soldier's blood, and some day he will be a soldier himself, and a brave one. I shall count on him for the Union," he said, with a smile.

Mrs. Stafford shook her head.

A few days later, Colonel Stafford, in accordance with an understanding, came over to General Denby's camp, and reported to be sent on to Washington as a prisoner of war. The General was absent on the lines at the time, but was

expected soon, and the Colonel waited for him at his headquarters. There had been many tears shed when his wife
bade him good-by.

About an hour after the Colonel arrived, the General and
his staff were riding back to camp along the road which ran
by the Holly Hill gate. Just before they reached it, two
little figures came out of the gate and started down the road.
One was a boy of five, who carried a toy sword, drawn, in
one hand, whilst with the other he led his companion, a little
girl of three, who clasped a large yellow-haired doll to her
breast.

The soldiers cantered forward and overtook them.

"Where are you going, my little people?" inquired the
General, gazing down at them affectionately.

"I'm goin' to get my papa," said the tiny swordsman
firmly, turning a sturdy and determined little face up to him.
"My mamma's cryin', an' I'm goin' to take my papa home.
I ain' goin' to let the Yankees have him."

The officers all broke into a murmur of mingled admira-
tion and amusement.

"No, we ain' goin' let the Yankees have our papa,"
chimed in Evelyn, pushing her tangled hair out of her eyes,
and keeping fast hold of Charlie's hand for fear of the horses
around her.

The General dismounted.

"How are you going to help, my little Semiramis?" he
asked, stooping over her with smiling eyes.

"I'm goin' to give my dolly if they will give me my papa," she said, gravely, as if she understood the equality of the exchange.

"Suppose you give a kiss instead?" There was a second of hesitation, and then she put up her little face, and the old General dropped on one knee in the road and lifted her in his arms, doll and all.

"Gentlemen," he said to his staff, "you behold the future defenders of the Union."

The little ones were coaxed home, and that afternoon, as Colonel Stafford was expecting to leave the camp for Washington with a lot of prisoners, a despatch was brought in to General Denby, who read it.

"Colonel," he said, addressing him, "I think I shall have to continue your parole a few days longer. I have just received information that, by a special cartel which I have arranged, you are to be exchanged for Colonel McDowell as soon as he can reach the lines at this point from Richmond; and meantime, as we have but indifferent accommodations here, I shall have to request you to consider Holly Hill as your place of confinement. Will you be so kind as to convey my respects to Mrs. Stafford, and to your young hero Bob, and make good my word to those two little commissioners of exchange, to whom I feel somewhat committed? I wish you a Merry Christmas and a Happy New Year."

"WHAT YOU CHILDREN GWINE DO WID DAT LITTLE CAT?" ASKED MAMMY, SEVERELY.

KITTYKIN, AND THE PART SHE PLAYED
IN THE WAR.

I.

KITTYKIN played a part in the war which has never been recorded. Her name does not appear in the list of any battle ; nor is she mentioned in any history as having saved a life, or as having done anything remarkable one way or the other. Yet, in fact, she played a most important part : she prevented a battle which was just going to begin, and brought about a truce between the skirmish lines of the Union and the Confederate troops near her home which lasted several weeks, and probably saved many lives.

There never was a kitten more highly prized than Kittykin, for Evelyn had long wanted a kitten, and the way she found her was so delightfully unexpected.

It was during the war, when everything was very scarce down in the South where Evelyn lived. "We don't have any coffee, or any kittens, or *any*thing," Evelyn said one day to some soldiers who had come to her home from their camp, which was a mile or so away. You would have thought from the way she put them together that kittens, like coffee, were something to have on the table ; but she had heard her mamma wishing for coffee at breakfast that morning, and she herself had long been wanting a kitten. Indeed, she used to ask for one in her prayers.

Evelyn had no fancy for anything that, in her own words, "was not live." A thing that had life was of more value in her eyes than all the toys that were ever given her. A young bird which, too fat to fly, had fallen from the nest, or a broken-legged chicken, which was too lame to keep up with its mother, had her tenderest care ; a little mouse slipping along the wainscot or playing on the carpet excited her liveliest interest ; but a kitten, a "real live kittykin," she had never possessed. though for a long time she had set her heart on having one. One day, however, she was out walking with her mammy in the "big road," when she met several small negro children coming along, and one of them had a little bit of a white kitten squeezed up in his arm. It looked very scared, and every now and then it cried "Mew, mew."

"Oh, mammy, look at that dear little kittykin!" cried Evelyn, running up to the children and stroking the little mite tenderly.

"What you children gwine do wid dat little cat?" asked mammy, severely.

"We gwine *loss* it," said the boy who had it, promptly.

"Oh, mammy, don't let them do that! Don't let them

hurt it!" pleaded Evelyn, turning to her mammy. "It would get so hungry."

A sudden thought struck her, and she sprang over toward the boy, and took the kitten from him, which instantly curled up in her arms just as close to her as it could get. There was no resisting her appeal, and a minute later she was running home far ahead of her mammy, with the kitten hugged tight in her arms. Her mamma was busy in the sitting-room when Evelyn came rushing in.

"Oh, mamma, see what I have! A dear little kittykin! Can't I have it? They were just going to throw it away, and lose it all by itself;" and she began to jump up and down and rub the kitten against her little pink cheek, till her mother had to take hold of her to quiet her excitement.

Kittykin (for that was the name she had received) must have misunderstood the action, and have supposed she was going to take her from her young mistress, for she suddenly bunched herself up into a little white ball, and gave such a spit at Evelyn's mamma that the lady jumped back nearly a yard, after which Kittykin quietly curled herself up again in Evelyn's arm. The next thing was to give her some warm milk, which she drank as if she had not had a mouthful all day; and then she was put to sleep in a basket of wool, where Evelyn looked at her a hundred times to see how she was coming on.

Evelyn never doubted after that that if she prayed for a thing she would get it; for she had been praying all the time for a "little white kitten," and not only was Kittykin as white as snow, but she was, to use Evelyn's words, "even littler" than she had expected. There could not, to her mind, be stronger proof.

As Kittykin grew a little she developed a temper entirely out of proportion to her size ; when she got mad, she got mad all over. If anything offended her she would suddenly back up into a corner, her tail would get about twice as large as usual, and she would spit like a little fury. However, she never fought her little mistress, and even in her worst moments she would allow Evelyn to take her and lay her on her back in the little cradle she had, or carry her by the neck, or the legs, or almost any way except by the tail. To pull her tail was a liberty she never would allow even Evelyn to take. If she was held by the tail her little pink claws flew out as quick as a wink and as sharp as needles. Evelyn was very kind to Kittykin, however, and was careful not to provoke her, for she had been told that getting angry and kicking on the floor, as she herself sometimes did when mammy wanted to comb her curly hair, would make an ugly little girl, and of course it would have the same effect on a kitten.

Fierce, however, as Kittykin was, it soon appeared that she was the greatest little coward in the world. A worm in the walk or a little beetle running across the floor would set her to jumping as if she had a fit, and the first time she ever saw a mouse she was far more afraid of it than it was of her. If it had been a rat, I am sure that she would have died.

One day Evelyn was sitting on the floor in her mother's chamber sewing a little blue bag, which she said was her work-bag, when a tiny mouse ran, like a little gray shadow, across the hearth. Kittykin was at the moment busily engaged in rolling about a ball of yarn almost as white as herself, and the first thing Evelyn knew she gave a jump like a trap-ball, and slid up the side of the bureau like a little shaft of light, where she stood with all four feet close together, her small back roached up in an arch, her tail all fuzzed up over it, and her mouth wide open and spitting like a little demon. She looked so funny that Evelyn dropped her sewing, and the mouse, frightened half out of its little wits, took advantage of her consternation to make a rush back to its hole under the wainscoting, into which it dived like a little duck. After holding her lofty position for some time, Kittykin let her hairs fall and lowered her back, but every now and then she would raise them again at the bare thought of the awful animal which had so terrified her. At length she decided that she might go down ; but how was she to do it ? Smooth though the mahogany was, she had, under excitement, gone up like a streak of lightning ; but now when she was cool she was afraid to jump down. It was so high that it made her head swim ; so, after walking timidly around and peeping over at the floor, she began to cry for some one to take her down, just as Evelyn would have done under the same circumstances.

Evelyn tried to coax her down, but she would not come ;

so finally she had to drag a chair up to the bureau and get up on it to reach her.

Perhaps it was the fright she experienced when she found herself up so high that caused Kittykin to revenge herself on the little mouse shortly afterward, or perhaps it was only her cat instinct developing; but it was only a short time after this that Kittykin did an act which grieved her little mistress dreadfully. The little mouse had lived under the wainscot since long before Kittykin had come, and it and Evelyn were on very good terms. It would come out and dash along by the wall to the wardrobe, under which it would disappear, and after staying there some time it would hurry back. This Evelyn used to call "paying visits;" and she often wondered what mice talked about when they got together under the wardrobe. Or sometimes it would slip out and frisk around on the floor—"just playing," as Evelyn said. There was a perfect understanding between them: Evelyn was not to hurt the mouse nor let mammy set a trap for it, and the mouse was not to bite Evelyn's clothes—but if it had to cut at all, was to confine itself to her mamma's. After Kittykin came, however, the mouse appeared to be much less sociable than formerly; and after the occasion when it alarmed Kittykin so, it did not come out again for a long time. Evelyn used to wonder if its mamma was keeping it in.

One day, however, Evelyn was sewing, and Kittykin was lying by, when she suddenly seemed to get tired of doing nothing, and began to walk about.

" Lie down, Kittykin," said her mistress ; but Kittykin did not appear to hear. She just lowered her head, and peeped under the bureau, with her eyes set in a curious way. Presently she stooped very low, and slid along the floor without making the slightest noise, every now and then stopping perfectly still. Evelyn watched her closely, for she had never seen her act so before. Suddenly, however, Kittykin gave a spring, and disappeared under the bureau. Evelyn heard a little squeak, and the next minute Kittykin walked out with a little mouse in her mouth, over which she was growling like a little tigress. Evelyn was jumping up to take it away from her when Kittykin, who had gone out into the middle of the room, turned it loose herself, and quietly walking away, lay down as if she were going to sleep. Then Evelyn saw that she did not mean to hurt it, so she sat and watched the mouse, which remained quite still for some time.

After a while it moved a little, to see if Kittykin was really asleep. Kittykin did not stir. Her eyes were fast shut, and the mouse seemed satisfied ; so, after waiting a bit, it made a little dash toward the bureau. In a single bound Kittykin was right over it, and had laid her white paw on it. She did not, however, appear to intend it any injury, but began to play with it just as Evelyn would have liked to do ; and, lying down, she rolled over and over, holding it up and tossing it gently, quite as Evelyn sometimes did her, or patting it and admiring it as if it had been the sweetest little mouse in the world. The mouse, too, appeared not to mind it the least bit; and Evelyn was just thinking how nice it was that Kitty-kin and it had become such friends, and was planning nice games with them, when there was a faint little squeak, and she saw Kittykin, who had just been petting the little crea-ture, suddenly drive her sharp white teeth into its neck.

Evelyn rushed at her.

"Oh, you wicked Kittykin! Aren't you ashamed of yourself?" she cried, catching her up by the tail and shak-ing her well, as the best way to punish her.

Just then her mamma entered. "Oh, Evelyn, why are you treating kitty so?" she asked.

"Because she's so mean," said Evelyn, severely. "She's a murderer."

Her mamma tried to explain that killing the mouse was Kittykin's nature; but Evelyn could not see that this made it any the less painful, and she was quite cool to Kittykin for some time.

The little mouse was buried that evening in a matchbox under a rose-bush in the garden; and Kittykin, in a black rag which was tied around her as a dress, was compelled, evi-dently much against her will, to do penance by acting as chief mourner.

KITTYKIN was about five months old when there was a
great marching of soldiers backward and forward ; the
tents in the field beyond the woods were taken down
and carried away in wagons, and there was an immense stir.
The army was said to be "moving." There were rumors
that the enemy was coming, and that there might be a battle
near there. Evelyn was so young that she did not understand any more of it than Kittykin did ; but her mother
appeared so troubled that Evelyn knew it was very bad,
and became frightened, though she did not know why. Her
mammy soon gave her such a gloomy account, that Evelyn
readily agreed with her that it was "like torment." As for
Kittykin, if she had been born in a battle, she could not have
been more unconcerned. In a day or two it was known that
the main body of the army was some little way off on a long
ridge, and that the enemy had taken up its position on
another hill not far distant, and Evelyn's home was between
them ; but there was no battle. Each army began to
intrench itself ; and in a little while there was a long red
bank stretched across the far edge of the great field behind
the house, which Evelyn was told was "breastworks" for the

4

picket line, and she pointed them out to Kittykin, who blinked and yawned as if she did not care the least bit if they were.

Next morning a small squadron of cavalry came galloping by. A body of the enemy had been seen, and they were going to learn what it meant. In a little while they came back.

"The enemy," they said, "were advancing, and there would probably be a skirmish right there immediately."

As they rode by, they urged Evelyn's mamma either to leave the house at once or to go down into the basement, where they might be safe from the bullets. Then they galloped on across the field to get the rest of their men, who were in the trenches beyond. Before they reached there a lot of men appeared on the edge of the wood in front of the house. No one could tell how many they were; but the sun gleamed on their arms, and there was evidently a good force. At first they were on horseback; but there was a "Bop! bop!" from the trenches in the field behind the house, and they rode back, and did not come out any more. Next morning, however, they too had dug a trench. These, Evelyn heard some one say, were a picket line. About eleven o'clock they came out into the field, and they seemed to have spread themselves out behind a little rise or knoll in front of the house. Mammy's teeth were just chattering, and she went to moaning and saying her prayers as hard as she could, and Evelyn's mamma told her to take Evelyn down into the basement, and she would bring the baby; so mammy, who had been following mamma about, seized Evelyn, and rushed with her down-stairs, where, although they were quite safe, as the windows were only half above the ground, she fell on her face on the floor, praying as if her last hour had come. "Bop! bop!" went some muskets up behind the house. "Bang! bop! bang!" went some on the other side.

Evelyn suddenly remembered Kittykin. "Where was she?" The last time she had seen her was a half-hour before, when she had been lying curled up on the back steps fast asleep in the sun. Suppose she should be there now, she would certainly be killed, for the back steps ran right out into the yard so as to be just the place for Kittykin to be shot. So thought Evelyn. "Bang! bang!" went the guns again—somewhere. Evelyn dragged a chair up to a window and looked. Her heart almost stopped; for there, out in the yard, quite clear of the houses, was Kittykin, standing some way up the trunk of a tall locust-tree, looking curiously around. Her little white body shone like a small patch of snow against the dark brown bark. Evelyn sprang down from the chair, and forgetting everything, rushed through the entry and out of doors.

"Kitty, kitty, kitty!" she called. "Kittykin, come here! You'll be killed! Come here, Kittykin!"

Kittykin, however, was in for a game, and as her little mistress, with her golden hair flying in the breeze, ran toward

her, she rushed scampering still higher up the tree.   Evelyn
could see that there were some men scattered out in the
fields on either side of her, some of them stooping, and some
lying down, and as she ran on toward the tree she heard a
" Bang ! bang !" on each side, and she saw little puffs of
white smoke, and something went "Zoo-ee-ee" up in the air ;
but she did not think about herself, she was so frightened for
Kittykin.

" Kitty, kitty !   Come down, Kittykin !" she called, running up to the tree and holding up her arms to her.   Kittykin might, perhaps, have liked to come down now, but she
could no longer do so ; she was too high up.   She looked
down, first over one shoulder, and then over the other, but it
was too high to jump.   She could not turn around, and her
head began to swim.   She grew so dizzy, she was afraid she
might fall, so she dug her little sharp claws into the bark,
and began to cry.

Evelyn would have run back to tell her mamma (who,
having sent the baby down-stairs to mammy, was still busy
up-stairs trying to hide some things, and so did not know she
was out in the yard); but she was so afraid Kittykin might
be killed that she could not let her get out of her sight.
Indeed, she was so absorbed in Kittykin that she forgot
all about everything else.   She even forgot all about the
soldiers.   But though she did not notice the soldiers, it
seemed that some of them had observed her.   Just as the
leader of the Confederate picket line was about to give an

"I WANT MY KITTYKIN," SAID EVELYN.

order to make a dash for the houses in the yard, to his hor-
ror he saw a little girl in a white dress and with flying hair
suddenly run out into the clear space right between him and
the soldiers on the other side, and stop under a tree just in
the line of their fire. His heart jumped into his mouth as he
sprang to his feet and waved his hands wildly to call attention to the child. Then shouting to his men to stop firing,
he walked out in front of the line, and came at a rapid stride
down the slope. The others all stood still and almost held
their breaths for fear some one would shoot; but no one did.
Evelyn was so busy trying to coax Kittykin down that she
did not notice anything until she heard some one call out :

" For Heaven's sake, run into the house, quick ! "

She looked around and saw the gentleman hurrying
toward her. He appeared to be very much excited.

" What on earth are you doing out here ? " he gasped, as
he came running up to her.

He was a young man, with just a little light mustache,
and with a little gold braid on the sleeves of his gray jacket ;
and though he seemed very much surprised, he looked very
kind.

" I want my Kittykin," said Evelyn, answering him, and
looking up the tree, with a little wave of her hand, towards
where Kittykin still clung tightly. Somehow she felt at the
moment that this gentleman could help her better than any
one else.

Kittykin, however, apparently thought differently about

it; for she suddenly stopped mewing; and as if she felt it
unsafe to be so near a stranger, she climbed carefully up
until she reached a limb, in the crotch of which she en-
sconced herself, and peeped curiously over at them with a
look of great satisfaction in her face, as much as to say,
"Now I'm safe. I'd like to see you get me."

The gentleman was stroking Evelyn's hair, and was
looking at her very intently, when a voice called to him
from the other side :

"Hello, Johnny! what's the matter?"

Evelyn looked around, and saw another gentleman coming
toward them. He was older than the first one, and had on a
blue coat, while the first had on a gray one. She knew one
was a Confederate and the other was a Yankee, and for a
second she was afraid they might shoot each other, but her
first friend called out :

"Her kitten is up the tree. Come ahead!"

He came on, and looked for a second up at Kittykin, but
he looked at Evelyn really hard, and suddenly stooped down,
and putting his arm around her, drew her up to him. She got
over her fear in a minute.

"Kittykin's up there, and I'm afraid she'll be kilt." She
waved her hand up over her head, where Kittykin was taking
occasion to put a few more limbs between herself and the
enemy.

"It's rather a dangerous place when the boys are out
hunting, eh, Johnny?" He laughed as he stood up again.

" Yes, for as big a fellow as you. You wouldn't stand the ghost of a show."

" I guess I'd feel small enough up there." And both men laughed.

By this time the men on both sides began to come up, with their guns over their arms.

" Hello ! what's up ?" some of them called out.

" Her kitten's up," said the first two ; and, to make good their words, Kittykin, not liking so many people below her, shifted her position again, and went up to a fresh limb, from which she again peeped over at them. The men all gathered around Evelyn, and began to talk to her, and both she and Kittykin were surprised to hear them joking and laughing together in the friendliest way.

" What are you doing out here ?" they asked ; and to all she made the same reply :

" I want my Kittykin."

Suddenly her mamma came out. She had just gone down-stairs, and had learned where Evelyn was. The two officers went up and spoke to her, but the men still crowded around Evelyn.

" She'll come down," said one. " All you have to do is to let her alone."

" No, she won't. She can't come down. It makes her head swim," said Evelyn.

" That's true," thought Kittykin up in the tree, and to let them understand it she gave a little " Mew."

"I don't see how anything can swim when it's as dry as it is around here," said a fellow in gray.

A man in blue handed him his canteen, which he at once accepted, and after surprising Evelyn by smelling it—which she knew was dreadfully bad manners—turned it up to his lips. She heard the liquid gurgling.

As he handed it back to its owner he said : "Yank, I'm mighty glad I didn't shoot you. I might have hit that canteen." At which there was a laugh, and the canteen went around until it was empty. Suddenly Kittykin from her high perch gave a faint "Mew," which said, as plainly as words could say it, that she wanted to get down and could not.

Evelyn's big brown eyes filled with tears. "I want my Kittykin," she said, her little lip trembling.

Instantly a dozen men unbuckled their belts, laid their guns on the ground, and pulled off their coats, each one trying to be the first to climb the tree. It was, however, too large for them to reach far enough around to get a good hold on it, so climbing it was found to be far more difficult than it looked to be.

"Why don't you cut it down?" asked some one.

But Evelyn cried out that that would kill Kittykin, so the man who suggested it was called a fool by the others. At last it was proposed that one man should stand against the tree and another should climb up on his shoulders, when he might get his arms far enough around it to work his way up. A stout fellow with a gray jacket on planted himself firmly against the trunk, and one who had taken off a blue jacket climbed up on his shoulders, and might have got up very well if he had not remarked that as the Johnnies had walked over him in the last battle, it was but fair that he should now walk over a Johnny. This joke tickled the man under him so that he slipped away and let him down. At length, however, three or four men got good "holds," and went slowly up one after the other amid such encouraging shouts from their friends on the ground below as : "Go it, Yank, the Johnny's almost got you !" "Look out, Johnny, the Yanks are right behind you !" etc., whilst Kittykin gazed down in astonishment from above, and Evelyn looked up breathless from below. With much pulling and kicking, four men finally got up to the lowest limb, after which the climbing was comparatively easy. A new difficulty, how-ever, presented itself. Kittykin suddenly took alarm, and retreated still higher up among the branches.

The higher they climbed after that, the higher she climbed, until she was away up on one of the topmost boughs, which was far too slender for any one to follow her. There she turned and looked back with alternate alarm and satisfaction expressed in her countenance. If the men stirred, she stood ready to fly ; if they kept still, she settled down and mewed plaintively. Once or twice as they moved she took fright and looked almost as if about to jump.

Evelyn was breathless with excitement. "Don't let her jump," she called, "she will get kilt !"

The men, too, were anxious to prevent that. They called
to her, held out their hands, and coaxed her in every tone by
which a kitten is supposed to be influenced. But it was all
in vain. No cajoleries, no promises, no threats, were of the
least avail. Kittykin was there safe, out of their reach, and
there she would remain, sixty feet above the ground. Suddenly she saw that something was occurring below. She saw
the men all gather around her little mistress, and could hear
her at first refuse to let something be done, and then consent.
She could not make out what it was, though she strained her
ears. She remembered to have heard mammy tell her little
mistress once that "curiosity had killed a cat," and she was
afraid to think too much about it so high up in the tree. Still
when she heard an order given, " Go back and get your blankets," and saw a whole lot of the men go running off into the
field on either side, and presently come back with their arms
full of blankets, she could not help wondering what they were
going to do. They at once began to unroll the blankets and
hold them open all around the tree, until a large circle of the
ground was quite hidden.

" Ah !" said Kittykin, " it's a wicked trap !" and she dug
her little claws deep into the bark, and made up her mind
that nothing should induce her to jump. Presently she heard
the soldiers in the tree under her call to those on the
ground :

" Are you ready ? "

And they said, " All right !"

"Ah!" said Kittykin, "they cannot get down, either. Serves them right!"

But suddenly they all waved their arms at her and cried, "Scat!"

Goodness! The idea of crying "scat" at a kitten when she is up in a tree!—"scat," which fills a kitten's breast with terror! It was brutal, and then it was all so unexpected. It came very near making her fall. As it was, it set her heart to thumping and bumping against her ribs, like a marble in a box. "Ah!" she thought, "if those brutes below were but mice, and I had them on the carpet!" So she dug her claws into the bark, which was quite tender up there, and it was well she did, for she heard some one call something below that sounded like "Shake!" and before she knew it the man nearest her reached up, and, seizing the limb on which she was, screwed up his face, and— Goodness! it nearly shook the teeth out of her mouth and the eyes out of her head.

Shake! shake! shake! it came again, each time nearly tearing her little claws out of their sockets and scaring her to death. She saw the ground swim far below her, and felt that she would be mashed to death. Shake! shake! shake! shake! She could not hold out much longer, and she spat down at them. How those brutes below laughed! She formed a desperate resolve. She would get even with them. "Ah, if they were but—" Shake! sha— With a fierce spit, partly of rage, partly of fear, Kittykin let go, whirled suddenly, and flung herself on the upturned face of the man next beneath

her, from him to the man below him, and finally, digging her
little claws deep in his flesh, sprang with a wild leap clear of
the boughs, and shot whizzing out into the air, whilst the two
men, thrown off their guard by the suddenness of the attack,
loosed their hold, and went crashing down into the forks upon
those below.

The first thing Evelyn and the men on the ground knew
was the crash of the falling men and the sight of Kittykin
coming whizzing down, her little claws clutching wildly at
the air. Before they could see what she was, she gave a
bounce like a trap-ball as high as a man's head, and then,
as she touched the ground again, shot like a wild sky-rocket
hissing across the yard, and, with her tail all crooked to
one side and as big as her body, vanished under the house.
Oh, such a shout as there was from the soldiers! Evelyn
heard them yelling as she ran off after Kittykin to see if
she wasn't dead. They fairly howled with delight as the
men in the tree, with scratched faces and torn clothes, came
crawling down. They looked very sheepish as they landed
among their comrades; but the question whether Kittykin
had landed in a blanket or had hit the solid ground fifty
feet out somewhat relieved them. They all agreed that she
had bounced twenty feet.

Why Kittykin was not killed outright was a marvel. One
of her eyes was a little bunged up, the claws on three of her
feet were loosened, and for a week she felt as if she had been
run through a sausage mill; but she never lost any of her

speed. Ever afterward when she saw a soldier she would run for life, and hide as far back under the house as she could get, with her eyes shining like two little live coals.

For some time, indeed, she lived in perpetual terror, for the soldiers of both lines used to come up to the house, as the friendship they formed that day never was changed, and though they remained on the two opposite hills for quite a while, they never fired a shot at each other. They used instead to meet and exchange tobacco and coffee, and laugh over the way Kittykin routed their joint forces in the tree the day of the skirmish.

As for Kittykin, she never put on any airs about it. She did not care for that sort of glory. She never afterward could tolerate a tree; the earth was good enough for her; and the highest she ever climbed was up in her little mistress's lap.

"NANCY PANSY."

I.

"NANCY PANSY" was what Middleburgh called her, though the parish register of baptism contained nothing nearer the name than that of one Anne, daughter of Baylor Seddon, Esq., and Ellenor his wife. Whatever the register may have thought about it, "Nancy Pansy" was what Middleburgh called her, and she looked so much like a cherub, with her great eyes laughing up at you and her tangles blowing all about her dimpling pink face, that Dr. Spotswood Hunter, or "the Old Doctor," as he was known to Middleburgh, used to vow she had gotten out of Paradise by mistake that Christmas Eve.

Nancy Pansy was the idol of the old doctor, as the old doctor was the idol of Middleburgh. He had given her a doll baby on the day she was born, and he always brought her one on her birthday, though, of course, the first three or four which he gave her were of rubber, because as long as she was a little girl she used to chew her doll after a most cannibal-like fashion, she and Harry's puppies taking turn and turn about at chewing in the most impartial and friendly way. Harry was the old doctor's son. As she grew a little older, however, the doctor brought her better dolls ; but the puppies got older faster than Nancy Pansy, and kept on chewing up her dolls, so they did not last very long, which, perhaps, was why she never had a "real live doll," as she called it.

Some people said the reason the old doctor was so fond of Nancy Pansy was because he had been a lover of her beautiful aunt, whose picture as Charity giving Bread to the Poor Woman and her Children was in the stained-glass window in the church, with the Advent angel in the panel below, to show that she had died at Christmas-tide and was an angel herself now ; some said it was because he had had a little daughter himself who had died when a wee bit of a girl, and Nancy Pansy reminded him of her ; some said it was because his youngest born, his boy Harry, with the light hair, who now commanded a company in the Army of North- ern Virginia, was so fond of Nancy Pansy's lovely sister Ellen ; some said it was because the old doctor was fond of all children ; but the old doctor said it was "because Nancy Pansy was Nancy Pansy," and looked like an angel, and had more sense than anybody in Middleburgh, except his old sorrel horse Slouch, who, he always maintained, had sense enough to have prevented the war if he had been consulted.

Whatever was the cause, Nancy Pansy was the old doc- tor's boon companion ; and wherever the old doctor was,

whether in his old rattling brown buggy, with Slouch jogging sleepily along the dusty roads which Middleburgh
called her "streets," or sitting in the shadiest corner of his
porch, Nancy Pansy was in her waking hours generally beside him, her great pansy-colored eyes and her sunny hair
making a bright contrast to the white locks and tanned
cheeks of the old man. His home was just across the fence
from the big house in which Nancy Pansy lived, and there
was a hole where two palings were pulled off, through which
Nancy Pansy used to slip when she went back and forth,
and through which her little black companion, whose name,
according to Nancy Pansy's dictionary, was "Marphy," just
could squeeze. Sometimes, indeed, Nancy Pansy used to
fall asleep over at the old doctor's on the warm summer
afternoons, and wake up next morning, curiously enough, to
find herself in a strange room, in a great big bed, with a railing around the top of the high bedposts, and curtains hanging from it, and with Marphy asleep on a pallet near by.

" That child is your shadow, doctor," said Nancy Pansy's
mother one day to him.

" No, madam ; she is my sunshine," answered the old
man, gravely.

Nancy Pansy's mother smiled, for when the old doctor
said a thing he meant it. All Middleburgh knew that, from
old Slouch, who never would open his eyes for any one else,
and old Mrs. Hippin, who never would admit she was better
to any one else, up to Nancy Pansy herself. Perhaps this

was the reason why when the war broke out, and all the
other men went into the army, the old doctor, who was too
old and feeble to go himself, but had sent his only son
Harry, was chosen by tacit consent as Middleburgh's general
adviser and guardian. Thus it was he who had to advise
Mrs. Latimer, the druggist's wife, how to keep the little
apothecary's shop at the corner of the Court-house Square
after her husband went into the army; and it was he who
advised Mrs. Seddon to keep the post-office in the little
building at the bottom of her lawn, which had served as her
husband's law office before he went off to the war at the head
of the Middleburgh Artillery. He even gave valuable assist-
ance as well as advice to Mrs. Hippin about curing her
chickens of the gapes; and to Nancy Pansy's great astonishment had several times performed a most remarkable oper-
ation by inserting a hair from old Slouch's mane down the
invalid's little stretched throat.

He used to go around the town nearly every afternoon,
seeing the healthy as well as the sick, and giving advice as
well as physic, both being taken with equal confidence. It
was what he called "reviewing his out-posts," and he used to
explain to Nancy Pansy that that was the way her father and
his Harry did in their camp. Nancy Pansy did not wholly
understand him, but she knew it was something that was just
right; so she nodded gravely, and said, "Umh-hmh!"

It was not hard to get a doll the first year of the war, but
before the second year was half over there was not one left

in Middleburgh. The old doctor explained to Nancy Pansy that they had all gone away to the war. She did not quite understand what dollies had to do with fighting, but she knew that war made the dolls disappear. Still she kept on talking about the new doll she would get on her birthday at Christmas, and as the old doctor used to talk to her about it, and discuss the sort of hair it should have, and the kind of dress it should wear, she never doubted that she should get it in her stocking as usual on Christmas morning.

II.

THE old doctor's boots were very bad—those old boots which Middleburgh knew as well as they knew Nancy Pansy's eyes or the church steeple. Mrs. Seddon had taken the trouble to scold him one day in the autumn when she heard him coughing, and she had sent him a small roll of money "on account," she wrote him, "of a long bill," to get a pair of new boots. The old doctor never sent in a bill; he would as soon have sent a small-pox patient into Nancy Pansy's play-room. He calmly returned the money, saying he never transacted business with women who had husbands, and that he had always dressed to suit himself, at which Mrs. Seddon laughed; for, like the rest of Middleburgh, she knew that those old boots never stood back for any weather, however bad. She arranged, however, to have a little money sent to him through the post-office from another town without any name to the letter enclosing it. But the old boots were still worn, and Nancy Pansy, at her mother's suggestion, learned to knit, that she might have a pair of yarn socks knit for the old doctor at Christmas. She intended to have kept this a secret, and she did keep it from every one but the doctor; she did not quite *tell* even him, but she could not help mak-

ing him "guess" about it. Christmas Eve she went over to
the old doctor's, and whilst she made him shut his eyes, hung
up his stocking herself, into which she poked a new pair of
very queer-shaped yarn socks, a little black in some places
from her little hands, for they were just done, and there had
not been time to wash them. She consulted the old doctor
to know if he really—really, "now, really"—thought Santa
Claus would bring her a doll "through the war;" but she
could only get a "perhaps" out of him, for he said he
had not heard from Harry.

It was about ten o'clock that night when the old doctor
came home from his round of visits, and opening his old
secretary, took out a long thin bundle wrapped in paper,
and slipping it into his pocket, went out again into the snow
which was falling. Old Limpid, the doctor's man, had taken
Slouch to the stable, so the old doctor walked, stumbling
around through the dark by the gate, thinking with a sigh
of his boy Harry, who would just have vaulted over the
palings, and who was that night sleeping in the snow somewhere. However, he smiled when he put the bundle into
Nancy Pansy's long stocking, and he smiled again when he
put his old worn boots to the fire and warmed his feet.
But when Nancy Pansy slipped next morning through her
"little doctor's-gate," as she called her hole in the fence, and
burst into his room before he was out of bed, to show him
with dancing eyes what Santa Claus had brought her, and
announced that she had "named her 'Harry,' all herself,"

the old doctor had to wipe his eyes before he could really
see her.

Harry was the first "real doll" Nancy Pansy had ever
had—that was what she said—and Harry soon became as
well known in Middleburgh as Nancy Pansy herself. She
used to accompany Nancy Pansy and the old doctor on their
rounds, and instead of the latter two being called "the
twins," they and Harry were now dubbed "the triplets." It
was astonishing what an influence Harry came to have on
Nancy Pansy's life. She carried her everywhere, and the
doll would frequently be seen sitting up in the old doctor's
buggy alone, whilst Slouch dozed in the sun outside of some
patient's door. Of course, so much work as Harry had to do
had the effect of marring her freshness a good deal, and
she met with one or two severe accidents, such as breaking her leg, and cracking her neck; but the old doctor
attended her in the gravest way, and performed such success-
ful operations that really she was, except as to looks, almost
as good as new; besides, as Nancy Pansy explained, dolls
had to have measles and "theseases" just like other folks.

III.

IN March, 186–, Middleburgh "fell." That is, it fell into
the hands of the Union army, and remained in their
hands afterwards. It was terrible at first, and Nancy
Pansy stuffed Harry into a box, and hid her away.

It was awfully lonesome, however, and to think of the
way Harry was doubled up and cramped down in that box
under the floor was dreadful. So at last, finding that whatever else they did, the soldiers did not trouble her, she took
Harry out. But she never could go about with her as
before, for of course things were different, and although she
got over her fright at the soldiers, as did her sister Ellen and
the rest of Middleburgh, they never were friendly. Indeed,
sometimes they were just the reverse, and at last they got to
such a pitch that the regiment which was there was taken
away, and a new regiment, or, rather, two new companies,
were sent there. These were Companies A and C of the
—th Regiment of —— Veterans. They had been originally
known as Volunteers, but now they were known as "Veterans," because they had been in so many battles.

The —th were perhaps the youngest men in that depart-
ment, being mainly young college fellows who had enlisted

all together. Some of the regiments composed of older men
were at first inclined to laugh at the smooth-faced youngsters
who could hardly raise a mustache to a mess; but when
these same rosy-cheeked fellows flung off their knapsacks in
battle after battle, and went rushing ahead under a hail of
bullets and shell, they changed their tune and dubbed them
"The Baby Veterans." Thus, in 186-, the Baby Veterans
went to Middleburgh for a double purpose :—first, that they
might recruit and rest; and, secondly, because for the past
six months Middleburgh had been causing much worry, and
was regarded as a nest of treason and trouble. The regiment which had been there before was a new regiment, not
long since recruited, and had been in a continual quarrel
with Middleburgh, and as Middleburgh consisted mainly of
women and children, and a few old men, there was not much
honor to be got out of rows with them. Middleburgh complained that the soldiers were tyrannical and caused the
trouble; the soldiers insisted that Middleburgh was constantly breaking the regulations, and conducted itself in a
high-handed and rebellious way, and treated them with open
scorn. As an evidence, it was cited that the women in
Middleburgh would not speak to the Union soldiers. And
it was rumored that the girls there were uncommonly pretty.
When the Baby Veterans heard this, they simply laughed,
pulled their budding mustaches, and announced that they
would " keep things straight in Middleburgh."

Tom Adams was first lieutenant of Company C. He

had enlisted as a private, and had been rapidly promoted to
corporal, sergeant, and then lieutenant ; and he was in a fair
way to be captain soon, as the captain of his company was
at home badly wounded, and if he should be permanently dis-
abled, Tom was certain of the captaincy. If any man could
bring Middleburgh to terms, Tom Adams was the man, so
his friends declared, and they would like to see any woman
who would refuse to speak to Tom Adams—they really
would.

The Baby Veterans reached Middleburgh in the night,
and took up their quarters on the Court-house Square, va-
cated by the regiment which had just left. When morning
came they took a look at Middleburgh, and determined to
intimidate it on the spot. They drilled, marched and
counter-marched up and down the dusty streets, and around
the old whitewashed court-house, to show that they meant
business, and did not propose to stand any foolishness—
not they.

Nancy Pansy and her sister Ellen had been with Harry
to see old Mrs. Hippin, who was sick, to carry her some
bread and butter, and were returning home about mid-day.
They had not seen the new soldiers, and were hurrying along,
hoping they might not see them, when they suddenly heard
the drums and fifes playing, and turning the corner, they saw
the soldiers between them and their gate, marching up the
road toward them. A tall young officer was at their head ;
his coat was buttoned up very tight, and he carried his drawn

sword with the handle in his right hand and the tip in his
left, and carried his head very high. It was Tom Adams.
Nancy Pansy caught tight hold of her sister's hand, and
clasped Harry closely to her bosom. For a second they
stopped; then, as there was no help for it, they started forward across the road, just in front of the soldiers. They
were so close that Nancy Pansy was afraid they would march
over them, and she would have liked to run. She clutched
sister's hand hard; but her sister did not quicken her pace at
all, and the young officer had to give the order, "Mark time
—march!" to let them pass. He looked very grand as
he drew himself up, but Nancy Pansy's sister held her hand
firmly, and took not the slightest notice of him. Lifting her
head defiantly in the air, and keeping her dark eyes straight
before her, she passed with Nancy Pansy within two steps
of the young lieutenant and his drawn sword, neither quick-
ening nor slowing her pace a particle. They might have
seemed not to know that a Federal soldier was within a
hundred miles of them but for the way that Nancy Pansy
squeezed Harry, and the scornful air which sat on her sister's
stern little face and erect figure as she drew Nancy Pansy
closer to her, and gathered up her skirts daintily in her small
hand, as though they might be soiled by an accidental
touch.

Tom Adams had a mind to give the order "Forward!"
and make them run out of the way, but he did not do it, so
he marched back to camp, and told the story to his mess,

NANCY PANSY CLASPED HARRY CLOSELY TO HER BOSOM.

W. L. Sheppard Del

walking around the table, holding the table-cloth in his hand,
to show how the little rebel had done. He vowed he would
get even with her.

As the days went on, the Baby Veterans and Middleburgh
came no nearer being acquainted than they were that morning. The Baby Veterans still drilled, and paraded, and set
pickets all around the town; Middleburgh and Nancy Pansy
still picked up their skirts and passed by with uplifted heads
and defiant eyes. The Baby Veterans shouted on the Court-
house Square, "Yankee Doodle" and the "Star-spangled
Banner;" Middleburgh sang on its verandas and in its par-
lors, "Dixie" and the "Bonnie Blue Flag." Perhaps, some
evenings Middleburgh may have stopped its own singing, and
have stolen out on its balconies to listen to the rich chorus
which came up from the Court-house Grove, but if so, the
Baby Veterans never knew it; or perhaps, the Baby Veterans
some evenings may have strolled along the shadowed streets,
or stretched themselves out on the grass to listen to the
sweet voices which floated down from the embowered verandas in the Judge's yard; if so, Middleburgh never guessed it.

Nancy Pansy used to sing sweetly, and she would often
sing whilst her sister played for her.

The strict regulations established by the soldiers prevented any letters from going or coming unopened, and
Middleburgh never would tolerate that. So the only mail
which passed through the office was that which the Baby
Veterans received or sent. As stated, Nancy Pansy's

mother, by the old doctor's advice and for reasons good
to her and her friends, still kept the post-office, under a
sort of surveillance, yet the intercourse with the soldiers
was strictly official; the letters were received or were delivered by the postmistress in silence, or if the Baby Veterans
asked a question it was generally replied to by a haughty
bow, or an ungracious " No."

One mail day Mrs. Seddon was ill, so Nancy Pansy's sister Ellen had to go to open the mail, and Nancy Pansy went
with her, taking Harry along, " to take care of them."

It happened that Tom Adams and a friend came in to ask
for their letters. Nancy Pansy's sister was standing at the
table arranging the mail, and Nancy Pansy was sitting up on
the table by her, holding the battered but cherished Harry in
her lap. The young officer stiffened up as he saw who was
before him.

" Are there any letters for Lieutenant Adams ? " he asked,
in a very formal and stately manner.

There was no reply or motion to show that he had been
heard, except that Nancy Pansy's sister began to go over the
letters again from the beginning of the A's. Suddenly Nancy
Pansy, who was watching her, saw one, and exclaiming, " Oh !
there's one ! " seized it, and slipped down from the table to
give it to its owner, proud to show that she could read writing. Before she had reached the window, however, her sister caught her quickly, and taking the letter from her, slowly
advanced and handed it to the young soldier; then turning

quietly away, she took out her handkerchief and wiped her hand very hard where it had touched the letter, as if it had been soiled. The young officer strode out of the door with a red face and an angry step, and that evening the story of the way the little rebel wiped her hands after touching Tom Adams's letter was all over camp.

6

IV.

AFTER this it was pretty well understood that the Baby Veterans and Middleburgh were at war. The regulations were more strictly enforced than ever before, and for a while it looked as if it was going to be as bad as it was when the other regiment was there. Old Limpid, the old doctor's man, was caught one night with some letters on his person, several of them addressed to "Captain Harry Hunter, Army of Northern Virginia," etc., and was somewhat severely dealt with, though, perhaps fortunately for him and his master, the letters, one of which was in a feminine hand, whilst abusive of the soldiers, did not contain any information which justified very severe measures, and after a warning he was set free again.

Nancy Pansy's sister Ellen was enraged next day to receive again her letter from a corporal's guard, indorsed with an official stamp, "Returned by order," etc. She actually cried about it.

Nancy Pansy had written a letter to Harry, too—not her own Harry, but the old doctor's—and hers came back also; but she did not cry about it, for she had forgotten to tell Harry that she had a kitten.

Still it was very bad ; for after that even the old doctor was once more subjected to the strict regulations which had existed before the Baby Veterans came, and he could no longer drive in and out at will, as he and Nancy Pansy had been doing since the regiment arrived.

It was not, however, long after this that Nancy Pansy had quite an adventure. She and Harry had been with the old doctor, and the old doctor had to go and see some children with the measles, so, as Harry had never had measles, he sent her and Nancy Pansy back; but Nancy Pansy had found an old cigar-box, which was a treasure, and would have made a splendid cradle for Harry, except that it was so short that when Harry's legs were put into it, her head and shoulders stuck up, and when her body was in it, her legs hung out. Still, if it would not do for a cradle, she had got a piece of string, and it would do for a carriage. So she was coming home very cheerfully, thinking of the way Harry would enjoy her ride down the walk.

It was just at this time that Tom Adams, feeling thoroughly bored with his surroundings, left camp and sauntered up the street alone, planning how he could get his company ordered once more to the front. He could not stand this life any longer. As he strolled along the walk the sound of the cheerful voices of girls behind the magnolias and rose bowers came to him, and a wave of homesickness swept over him as he thought of his sisters and little nieces away up North.

Suddenly, as he turned a corner, he saw a small figure walking slowly along before him ; the great straw hat on the back of her head almost concealed the little body, but her sunny hair was peeping down below the broad brim, and Adams knew the child.

She carried under her arm an old cigar-box, out of one end of which peeped the head and shoulders of an old doll, the feet of which stuck out of the other end. A string hung from the box, and trailed behind her on the pathway. She appeared to be very busy about something, and to be per-fectly happy, for as she walked along she was singing out of her content a wordless little song of her heart, " Tra-la-la, tra-la-la."

The young officer fell into the same gait with the child, and instinctively trod softly to keep from disturbing her. Just then, however, a burly fellow named Griff O'Meara, who had belonged to one of the companies which preceded them, and had been transferred to Adams's company, came down a side street, and turned into the walkway just behind the little maid. He seemed to be tipsy. The trailing string caught his eye, and he tipped forward and tried to step on it. Adams did not take in what the fellow was trying to do until he attempted it the second time. Then he called to him, but it was too late ; he had stepped on the cord, and jerked the box, doll and all, from the child's arm. The doll fell, face down, on a stone and broke to pieces. The man gave a great laugh, as the little girl turned, with a cry of anguish,

and stooping, began to pick up the fragments, weeping in a
low, pitiful way. In a second Adams sprang forward, and
struck the fellow a blow between the eyes which sent him
staggering off the sidewalk, down in the road, flat on his
back. He rose with an oath, but Adams struck him a
second blow which laid him out again, and the fellow, finding him to be an officer, was glad to slink off. Adams then
turned to the child, whose tears, which had dried for a
moment in her alarm at the fight, now began to flow again
over her doll.

"Her pretty head's all broke! Oh—oh—oh!" she
sobbed, trying vainly to get the pieces to fit into something
like a face.

The young officer sat down on the ground by her.
"Never mind, sissy," he said, soothingly, "let me see if I can
help you."

She confidingly handed him the fragments, whilst she
tried to stifle her sobs, and wiped her eyes with her little
pinafore.

"Can you do it?" she asked, dolefully, behind her pinafore.

"I hope so. What's your name?"

"Nancy Pansy, and my dolly's named Harry."

"Harry!" Tom looked at the doll's dress and the fragments of face, which certainly were not masculine.

"Yes, Harry Hunter. He's my sweetheart," she looked
at him to see that he understood her.

"Ah!"

"And sister's," she nodded, confidently.

"Yes, I see. Where is he?"

"He's a captain now. He's gone away—away." She waved her hand in a wide sweep to give an idea of the great distance it was. "He's in the army."

"Come along with me," said Tom; "let's see what we can do." He gathered up all the broken pieces in his handkerchief, and set out in the direction from which he had come, Nancy Pansy at his side. She slipped her little hand confidingly into his.

"You knocked that bad man down for me, didn't you?" she said, looking up into his face. Tom had not felt until then what a hero he had been.

"Yes," he said, quite graciously. The little warm fingers worked themselves yet further into his palm.

At the corner they turned up the street toward the Courthouse Square, and in a few minutes were in camp. At the sight of the child with Adams the whole camp turned out pell-mell, as if the "long-roll" had beat.

At first Nancy Pansy was a little shy, there was so much excitement, and she clung tightly to Tom Adams's hand. She soon found, however, that they were all friendly.

Tom conducted her to his tent, where she was placed in a great chair, with a horse-cover over it, as a sort of throne. The story of O'Meara's act excited so much indignation that Tom felt it necessary to explain fully the punishment he had given him.

Nancy Pansy, feeling that she had an interest in the matter, suddenly took up the narrative.

"Yes, he jus' knocked him down," she said, with the most charming confidence, to her admiring audience, her pink cheeks glowing and her great eyes lighting up at the recital, as she illustrated Tom's act with a most expressive gesture of her by no means clean little fist.

The soldiers about her burst into a roar of delighted laughter, and made her tell them again and again how it was done, each time renewing their applause over the 'cute way in which she imitated Tom's act. Then they all insisted on being formally introduced, so Nancy Pansy was stood upon the table, and the men came by in line, one by one, and were presented to her. It was a regular levee.

Presently she said she must go home, so she was taken down ; but before she was allowed to leave, she was invited to go through the camp, each man insisting that she should visit his tent. She made, therefore, a complete tour, and in every tent some souvenir was pressed upon her, or she was begged to take her choice of its contents. Thus, before she had gone far, she had her arms full of things, and a string of men were following her bearing the articles she had honored them by accepting. There were little looking-glasses, pin-cushions, pairs of scissors, pictures, razors, bits of gold-lace, cigar-holders, scarf-pins, and many other things.

When she left camp she was quite piled up with things, whilst Tom Adams, who acted as her escort, marched behind

her with a large basketful besides. She did not have room
to take Harry, so she left her behind, on the assurance of
Tom that she should be mended, and on the engagement of
the entire company to take care of her. The soldiers followed her to the edge of the camp, and exacted from her a
promise to come again next day, which she agreed to do if
her mother would let her. And when she was out of sight,
the whole command held a council of war over the fragments
of Harry.

When Adams reached the Judge's gate he made a negro
who was passing take the basket in, thinking it better not to
go himself up to the house. He said good-by, and Nancy
Pansy started up the walk, whilst he waited at the gate.
Suddenly she turned and came back.

" Good-by !" she said, standing on tiptoe, and putting up
her little face to be kissed.

The young officer stooped over the gate and kissed her.

"Good-by ! Come again to-morrow."

"Yes, if mamma will let me." And she tripped away
with her armful of presents.

Tom Adams remained leaning on the gate. He was
thinking of his home far away. Suddenly he was aroused by
hearing the astonished exclamations in the house as Nancy
Pansy entered. He felt sure that they were insisting that
the things should be sent back, and fearing that he might be
seen, he left the spot and went slowly back to camp, where
he found the soldiers still in a state of pleasurable excite-

ment over Nancy Pansy's visit. A collection was taken up for a purpose which appeared to interest everybody, and a cap nearly full of money was delivered to Tom Adams, with as many directions as to what he was to do with it as though it were to get a memorial for the Commander-in-chief. Tom said he had already determined to do the very same thing himself; still, if the company wished to "go in" with him, they could do it; so he agreed to take the money.

V.

ON the day following Nancy Pansy's visit to the camp
of the Baby Veterans, Adams took to the post-office
a bundle addressed to "Nancy Pansy," and a letter
addressed to a friend of his who was in Washington. The
bundle contained "Harry," as fully restored as her shattered
state would admit of; the letter contained a draft and a
commission, the importance of which latter Captain Adams
had put in the very strongest light.

He held his head very high as he dropped his letter into
the box, for over the table bent the slender figure of the
little dark-eyed postmistress, who had wiped her dainty
fingers so carefully after handling his letter. Perched near
her on the table, just as she had been that day, with her
tangled hair all over her face, was Nancy Pansy. She was,
as usual, very busy over something; but, hearing a step, she
glanced up.

"Oh, there's Tom Adams!" she exclaimed; and, turning
over on her face, she slipped down from the table and ran
up to him, putting up her face to be kissed, just as she
always did to the old doctor.

Adams stooped over and kissed her, though, as he did

SHE RAN UP TO HIM, PUTTING UP HER FACE TO BE KISSED.

so, he heard her sister turn around, and he felt as if she might be going to shoot him in the back. He straightened up with defiance in his heart. She was facing him ; but what was his astonishment when she advanced, and with a little smile on her lovely face, said :

"Captain Adams, I am Miss Seddon. My mother has desired me to thank you in her name, and in all our names, for your act of protection to my little sister on yesterday."

"Yes," said Nancy Pansy; "he jus' knocked that bad man down," and she gave her little head a nod of satisfaction to one side.

The young officer blushed to his eyes. He was prepared for an attack, but not for such a flank movement. He stammered something about not having done anything at all worthy of thanks, and fell back behind Harry, whom he suddenly pulled out and placed in Nancy Pansy's hands. It all ended in an invitation from Mrs. Seddon, through Nancy Pansy and her pretty sister, to come up to the house and be thanked, which he accepted.

After this the Baby Veterans and Middleburgh came to understand each other a good deal better than before. Instead of remaining in their camp or marching up and down the streets, with arrogance or defiance stamped on every face and speaking from every figure, the Baby Veterans took to loafing about town in off-duty hours, hanging over the gates, or sauntering in the autumn twilight up and down the quiet walks. They and Middleburgh

still recognized that there was a broad ground, on which
neither could trespass. The Baby Veterans still sang "The
Star-spangled Banner" in the Court-house Grove, and
Middleburgh still sang "Dixie" and the "Bonnie Blue
Flag" behind her rose trellises; but there was no more
gathering up of skirts, and disdainful wiping of hands after
handling letters; and the old doctor was allowed to go
jogging about on his rounds, with Nancy Pansy and the
scarred Harry at his side, as unmolested as if the Baby
Veterans had never pitched their tents on the Court-house
Square. It is barely possible that even the rigid invest-
ment of the town relaxed a little as the autumn changed
into winter, for once or twice old Limpid disappeared for
several days, as he used to do before his arrest, and Nancy
Pansy's pretty sister used to get letters from Harry, who
was now a major. Nancy Pansy heard whispers of Harry's
coming before long, and even of the whole army's coming.
Somehow a rumor of this must have reached the authori-
ties, though Nancy Pansy never breathed a word of it; for
an officer was sent down to investigate the matter and
report immediately.

Just as he arrived he received secret word from some one
that a rebel officer was actually in Middleburgh.

That afternoon Nancy Pansy was playing in the bottom
of the yard when a lot of soldiers came along the street,
and before them rode a strange, cross-looking man with a
beard. Tom Adams was marching with the soldiers, and

he did not look at all pleased. They stopped at the old doctor's gate, and the strange man trotted up to her place and asked Nancy Pansy if she knew Captain Harry Hunter.

"Yes, indeed," said Nancy Pansy, going up to the fence and poking her little rosy face over it; "Harry's a major now."

"Ah! Harry's a major now, is he?" said the strange man.

Nancy Pansy went on to tell him how her Harry was named after the other Harry, and how she was all broken now; but the officer was intent on something else.

"Where is Harry now?" he asked her.

"In the house," and she waved her hand toward the old doctor's house behind her.

"So, so," said the officer, and went back to Tom Adams, who looked annoyed, and said:

"I don't believe it; there's some mistake."

At this the strange man got angry and said: "Lieutenant Adams, if you don't want the rebel caught, you can go back to camp."

My! how angry Tom was! His face got perfectly white, and he said: "Major Black, you are my superior, or you wouldn't dare to speak so to me. I have nothing to say now, but some day I'll out-rank you."

Nancy Pansy did not know what they were talking about, but she did not like the strange man at all; so when he asked her: "Won't you show me where Harry

is?" at first she said "No," and then "Yes, if you won't
hurt him."

"No, indeed," said the man. As Tom Adams was there
she was not afraid; so she went outside the gate and on
into the old doctor's yard, followed by the soldiers and Tom
Adams, who still looked angry, and told her she'd better run
home. Some of the soldiers went around behind the house.

"Where is he?" the strange gentleman asked.

"Asleep up-stairs in the company-room," said Nancy
Pansy in a whisper. "You mustn't make any noise."

She opened the door and they entered the house, Nancy
Pansy on tiptoe and the others stepping softly. She was
surprised to see the strange man draw a pistol; but she
was used to seeing pistols, so, though Tom Adams told her
again to run home, she stayed there.

"Which is the company-room?" asked the strange man.

She pointed to the door at the head of the steps.
"That's it."

He turned to the soldiers.

"Come ahead, men," he said, in a low voice, and ran
lightly up the stairs, looking very fierce. When he reached
the door he seized the knob and dashed into the room.

Then Nancy Pansy heard him say some naughty words,
and she ran up the stairs to see what was the matter.

They were all standing around the big bed on which
she had laid Harry an hour before, with her head on a
pillow; but a jerk of the counterpane had thrown Harry

over on her face, and her broken neck and ear looked very bad.

"Oh, you've waked her up!" cried Nancy Pansy, rushing forward, and turning the doll over.

The strange man stamped out of the room, looking perfectly furious, and the soldiers all laughed. Tom Adams looked pleased.

7

VI

WHEN Tom Adams next called at the Judge's, he found the atmosphere much cooler within the house than it was outside. He had been waiting alone in the drawing-room for some time when Nancy Pansy entered. She came in very slowly, and instead of running immediately up to him and greeting him as she usually did, she seated herself on the edge of a chair and looked at him with manifest suspicion. He stretched out his hand to her.

" Come over, Nancy Pansy, and sit on my knee."

Nancy Pansy shook her head.

" My sister don't like you," she said slowly, eying him askance.

" Ah !" He let his hand fall on the arm of the chair.

" No ; and I don't, either," said Nancy Pansy, more confidently.

" Why doesn't she like me ?" asked Tom Adams.

" Because you are so mean. She says you are just like all the rest of 'em ;" and, pleased at her visitor's interest, Nancy Pansy wriggled herself higher up on her chair, prepared to give him further details.

" We don't like you at all," said the child, half confidentially and half defiantly. "We like our side; we like *Confederates.*" Tom Adams smiled. "We like Harry; we don't like you."

She looked as defiant as possible, and just then a step was heard in the hall, approaching very slowly, and Nancy Pansy's sister appeared in the doorway. She was dressed in white, and she carried her head even higher than usual.

The visitor rose. He thought he had never seen her look so pretty.

"Good-evening," he said.

She bowed "Good-evening," very slowly, and took a seat on a straight-backed chair in a corner of the room, ignoring the chair which Adams offered her.

"I have not seen you for some time," he began.

"No; I suppose you have been busy searching people's houses," she said.

Tom Adams flushed a little.

"I carry out my orders," he said. "These I must enforce."

"Ah!"

Nancy Pansy did not just understand it all, but she saw there was a battle going on, and she at once aligned herself with her side, and going over, stood by her sister's chair, and looked defiance at the enemy.

"Well, we shall hardly agree about this, so we won't discuss it," said Tom Adams. "I did not come to talk about this, but to see you, and to get you to sing for me."

Refusal spoke so plainly in her face that he added : " Or,
if you won't sing, to get Nancy Pansy to sing for me."

" *I* won't sing for you," declared Nancy Pansy, promptly
and decisively.

" What incorrigible rebels all of you are !" said Tom
Adams, smiling. He was once more at his ease, and he
pulled his chair up nearer Nancy Pansy's sister, and caught
Nancy Pansy by the hand. She was just trying to pull
away, when there were steps on the walk outside—the
regular tramp, tramp of soldiers marching in some num-
bers. They came up to the house, and some order was
given in a low tone. Both Adams and Nancy Pansy's
sister sprang to their feet.

" What can it mean ? " asked Nancy Pansy's sister, more
to herself than to Adams.

He went into the hall just as there was a loud rap at
the front door.

" What is it ? " he asked the lieutenant who stood there.

" Some one has slipped through the lines, and is in this
house," he said.

Nancy Pansy's sister stepped out into the hall.

" There is no one here," she said. She looked at Tom
Adams. " I give my word there is no one in the house
except my mother, ourselves, and the servants." She met
Tom Adams's gaze frankly as he looked into her eyes.

" There is no one here, Hector," he said, turning to the
officer.

"This is a serious matter," began the other, hesitatingly. "We have good grounds to believe——"

"I will be responsible," said Tom Adams, firmly. "I have been here some time, and there is no one here." He took the officer aside and talked to him a moment.

"All right," said he, as he went down the steps, "as you are so positive."

"I am," said Tom.

The soldiers marched down the walk, out of the gate, and around the corner. Just as the sound of their footsteps died away on the soft road, Tom Adams turned and faced Nancy Pansy's sister. She was leaning against a pillar, looking down, and a little moonlight sifted through the rose-bushes and fell on her neck. Nancy Pansy had gone into the house. "I am sorry I said what I did in the parlor just now." She looked up at him.

"Oh!" said Tom Adams, and moved his hand a little. "I——" he began; but just then there was a sudden scamper in the hall, and Nancy Pansy, with flying hair and dancing eyes, came rushing out on the portico.

"Oh, sister!" she panted. "Harry's come; he's in mamma's room!"

Nancy Pansy's sister turned deadly white. "Oh, Nancy Pansy!" she gasped, placing her hand over her mouth.

Nancy Pansy burst into tears, and buried her face in her sister's dress. She had not seen Tom Adams; she thought he had gone.

"I did not know it," said Nancy Pansy's sister, turning and facing Tom Adams's stern gaze.

"I believe you," he said, slowly. He felt at his side; but he was in a fatigue suit, and had no arms. Without finishing his sentence he sprang over the railing, and with a long, swift stride went down the yard. She dimly saw him as he sprang over the fence, and heard him call, "Oh, Hector!"

As he did so, she rushed into the house. "Fly! they are coming!" she cried, bursting into her mother's room. "Oh, Harry, they are coming!" she cried, rushing up to a handsome young fellow, who sprang to his feet as she entered, and went forward to meet her.

The young man took her hand and drew her to him. "Well," he said, looking down into her eyes, and drawing a long breath.

Nancy Pansy's sister put her face on his shoulder and began to cry, and Nancy Pansy rushed into her mother's arms and cried too.

Ten minutes later soldiers came in both at the front and back doors. Mrs. Seddon met her visitors in the hall. Nancy Pansy's sister was on one side, and Nancy Pansy on the other.

Tom Adams was in command. He removed his hat, but said, gravely: "I must arrest the young rebel officer who is here."

Nancy Pansy made a movement; but her mother tightened her clasp of her hand.

" Yes," she said, bowing. That was all.

Guards were left at the doors, and soldiers went through the house. The search was thorough, but the game had escaped. They were coming down the steps when some one said :

" We must search the shrubbery ; he will be there."

" No ; he is at his father's—the old doctor's," said Adams.

It was said in an undertone, but Mrs. Seddon's face whitened ; Nancy Pansy caught it, too. She clutched her mother's gown.

" Oh, mamma ! you hear what he says ? "

Her mother stooped and whispered to her.

" Yes, yes," nodded Nancy Pansy. She ran to the door, and poking her little head out, looked up and down the portico, calling, " Kitty, kitty ! "

The sentry who was standing there holding his gun moved a little, and, leaning out, peered into the dusk.

" 'Tain't out here," he said, in a friendly tone.

Nancy Pansy slipped past him, and went down the steps and around the portico, still calling, " Kitty ! Kitty ! Kitty !"

" Who goes there ? " called a soldier, as he saw something move over near the old doctor's fence ; but when he heard a childish voice call, " Kitty ! Kitty !" he dropped his gun again with a laugh. " 'Tain't nobody but that little gal, Nancy Pansy ; blest if I wa'n't about to shoot her !"

The next instant Nancy Pansy had slipped through her little hole in the fence, through which she had so often gone, and was in the old doctor's yard ; and when, five minutes afterward, Tom Adams marched his men up the walk and surrounded and entered the house, Nancy Pansy, her broken doll in her arms, was sitting demurely on the edge of a large chair, looking at him with great, wide-open, dancing eyes.   A little princess could not have been grander, and if she had hidden Harry Hunter behind her chair, she could not have shown more plainly that she had given him warning.

VII.

ALL Middleburgh knew next day how Nancy Pansy had saved Harry Hunter, and it was still talking about it, when it was one morning astonished by the news that old Dr. Hunter had been arrested in the night by the soldiers, who had come down from Washington, and had been carried off somewhere. There had not been such excitement since the Middleburgh Artillery had marched away to the war. The old doctor was sacred. Why, to carry him off, and stop his old buggy rattling about the streets, was, in Middleburgh's eyes, like stopping the chariot of the sun, or turning the stars out of their courses. Why did they not arrest Nancy Pansy too? asked Middleburgh. Nancy Pansy cried all day, and many times after, whenever she thought about it. She went to Tom Adams's camp and begged him to bring her old doctor back, and Tom Adams said as he had not had him arrested he could not tell what he could do, but he would do all he could. Then she wrote the old doctor a letter. However, all Middleburgh would not accept Tom Adams's statement as Nancy Pansy did, and instead of holding him as a favorite, it used to speak of him as " That Tom

Adams." Every old woman in Middleburgh declared she
was worse than she had been in ten years, and old Mrs.
Hippin took to her crutch, which she had not used in twelve
months, and told Nancy Pansy's sister she would die in a
week unless she could hear the old doctor's buggy rattle
again.   But when the fever broke out in the little low
houses down on the river, things began to look very serious.   The surgeon from the camp went to see the patients,
but they died, and more were taken ill.   When a number
of other cases occurred in the town itself, all of the most
malignant type, the surgeon admitted that it was a form
of fever with which he was not familiar.   There had never
been such an epidemic in Middleburgh before, and Middleburgh said that it was all due to the old doctor's absence.

One day Nancy Pansy went to the camp, to ask about the
old doctor, and saw a man sitting astride of a fence rail which
was laid on two posts high up from the ground.   He had a
stone tied to each foot, and he was groaning.   She looked up
at him, and saw that it was the man who had broken her
doll.   She was about to run away, but he groaned so she
thought he must be in great pain, and that always hurt her ;
so she went closer, and asked him what was the matter.   She
did not understand just what he said, but it was something
about the weight on his feet ; so she first tried to untie
the strings which held the stones, and then, as there was a
barrel standing by, she pushed at it until she got it up close
under him, and told him to rest his feet on that, whilst she

ran home and asked her mamma to lend her her scissors.
In pushing the barrel she broke Harry's head in pieces ;
but she was so busy she did not mind it then.   Just as she
got the barrel in place some one called her, and turning
around she saw a sentinel ; he told her to go away, and he
kicked the barrel from under the man and let the stones
drop down and jerk his ankles again.   Nancy Pansy began
to cry, and ran off up to Tom Adams's tent and told him
all about it, and how the poor man was groaning   Tom
Adams tried to explain that this man had got drunk, and
that he was a bad man, and was the same one who had
broken her doll.   It had no effect.   " Oh, but it hurts him
so bad ! " said Nancy Pansy, and she cried until Tom
Adams called a man and told him he might go and let
O'Meara down, and tell him that the little girl had begged
him off this time.   Nancy Pansy, however, ran herself, and
called to him that Tom Adams said he might get down.
When he was on the ground, he walked up to her and said :

"May the Holy Virgin kape you !   Griff O'Meara'll
never forgit you."

A few days after that, Nancy Pansy complained of head-
ache, and her mother kept her in the house.   That evening her face was flushed, and she had a fever ; so her
mother put her to bed and sat by her.   She went to sleep,
but waked in the night, talking very fast.   She had a burn-
ing fever, and was quite out of her head.   Mrs. Seddon
sent for the surgeon next morning, and he came and stayed

some time. When he returned to camp he went to Tom
Adams's tent. He looked so grave as he came in that
Adams asked quickly :

"Any fresh cases?"

"Not in camp." He sat down.

"Where?"

"That little girl—Nancy Pansy."

Tom Adams's face turned whiter than it had ever turned
in battle.

"Is she ill?"

"Desperately."

Tom Adams sprang to his feet.

"How long—how long can she hold out?" he asked, in
a broken voice.

"Twenty-four hours, perhaps," said the surgeon.

Tom Adams put on his cap and left the tent. Five
minutes later he was in the hall at the Judge's. Just as
he entered, Nancy Pansy's sister came quickly out of a
door. She had been crying.

"How is she? I have just this instant heard of it,"
said Tom, with real grief in his voice.

She put her handkerchief to her eyes.

"So ill," she sobbed.

"Can I see her?" asked Tom, gently.

"Yes; it won't hurt her."

When Tom Adams entered the room he was so shocked
that he stopped still. Mrs. Seddon bent over the bed with

her face pale and worn, and in the bed lay Nancy Pansy,
so changed that Tom Adams never would have known
her. She had fallen off so in that short time that he
would not have recognized her. Her face was perfectly
white, except two bright red spots on her cheeks. She
was drawing short, quick breaths, and was talking all the
time very fast. No one could understand just what she
was saying, but a good deal of it was about Harry and
the old doctor. Tom bent over her, but she did not know
him ; she just went on talking faster than ever.

"Nancy Pansy, don't you know Tom Adams?" her
mother asked her, in a soothing voice. She had never
called the young man so before, and he felt that it gave
him a place with Nancy Pansy ; but the child did not know
him ; she said something about not having any Harry.

"She is growing weaker," said her mother.

Tom Adams leaned over and kissed the child, and left
the room.

As he came down the steps he met Griff O'Meara, who
asked how the "little gurl" was, "bless her sowl!" When
he told him, Griff turned away and wiped his eyes with
the back of his hand. Tom Adams told him to stay there
and act as guard, which Griff vowed he'd do if the "howl
ribel army kem."

Ten minutes later Tom galloped out of camp with a
paper in his pocket signed by the surgeon. In an hour he
had covered the twelve miles of mud which lay between

Middleburgh and the nearest telegraph station, and was sending a message to General ———, his commander. At last an answer came. Tom Adams read it.

"Tell him it is a matter of life and death," he said to the operator. "Tell him there is no one else who understands it and can check it, and tell him it must be done before the afternoon train leaves, or it will be too late. Here, I'll write it out." And he did so, putting all his eloquence into the despatch.

Late that night two men galloped through the mud and slush in the direction of Middleburgh. The younger one had a large box before him on his horse; the other was quite an old man. Picket after picket was passed with a word spoken by the younger man, and they galloped on. At last they stopped at the Judge's gate, and sprang from their splashed and smoking horses.

As they hurried up the walk, the guard at the steps challenged them in a rich Irish brogue.

"It's I, O'Meara. You here still? How is she?"

"'Most in the Holy Virgin's arms," said the Irishman.

"Is she alive?" asked both men.

"It's a docther can tell that," said the sentinel. "They thought her gone an hour ago. There's several in there," he said to his captain. "I didn't let 'em in at firrst, but the young leddy said they wuz the frien's of the little gurl, an' I let 'em by a bit."

A minute later the old man entered the sick-room, whilst

Tom Adams stopped at the door outside. There was a general cry as he entered of, "Oh, doctor!"

And Mrs. Seddon called him: "Quick, quick, doctor! she's dying!"

"She's dead," said one of the ladies who stood by.

The old doctor bent over the little still white form, and his countenance fell. She was not breathing. With one hand he picked up her little white arm and felt for the pulse; with the other he took a small case from his pocket. "Brandy," he said. It was quickly handed him. He poured some into a little syringe, and stuck it into Nancy Pansy's arm, by turns holding her wrist and feeling over her heart.

Presently he said, quietly, "She's living," and both Mrs. Seddon and Nancy Pansy's sister said, "Thank God!"

All night long the old doctor worked over Nancy Pansy. Just before dawn he said to Mrs. Seddon: "What day is this?"

"Christmas morning," said Mrs. Seddon.

"Well, madam, I hope God has answered your prayers, and given your babe back to you; I hope the crisis is passed. Have you hung up her stocking?"

"No," said Nancy Pansy's mother. "She was so—" She could not say anything more. Presently she added: "She was all the time talking about you and Harry."

The old doctor rose and went out of the room. It was about dawn. He left the house, and went over to his own home. There, after some difficulty, he got in, and went to

his office. His old secretary had been opened and papers
taken out, but the old man did not seem to mind it. Pulling
the secretary out from the wall, he touched a secret spring.
It did not work at first, but after a while it moved, and he
put his hand under it, and pulled out a secret drawer. In it
were a number of small parcels carefully tied up with pieces
of ribbon, which were now quite faded, and from one peeped
a curl of soft brown hair, like that of a little girl. The old
doctor laid his fingers softly on it, and his old face wore a
gentle look. The largest bundle was wrapped in oil-silk.
This he took out and carefully unwrapped. Inside was yet
another wrapping of tissue paper. He put the bundle, with
a sigh, into his overcoat pocket, and went slowly back to the
Judge's. Nancy Pansy was still sleeping quietly.

The old doctor asked for a stocking, and it was brought
him. He took the bundle from his pocket, and, unwrapping
it, held it up. It was a beautiful doll, with yellow hair done
up with little tucking combs such as ladies used to wear, and
with a lovely little old tiny-flowered silk dress.

"She is thirty years old, madam," he said gently to Mrs.
Seddon, as he slipped the doll into the stocking, and hung it
on the bed-post. "I have kept her for thirty years, thinking I could never give it to any one ; but last night I knew
I loved Nancy Pansy enough to give it to her." He leaned
over and felt her pulse. "She is sleeping well," he said.

Just then the door opened, and in tipped Tom Adams,
followed by Griff O'Meara in his stocking feet, bearing a

large baby-house fitted up like a perfect palace, with every room carpeted and furnished, and with a splendid doll sitting on a balcony.

"A Christmas gift to that blessed angel from the Baby Veterans, mem," he said, as he set it down ; and then taking from his bulging pocket a large red-cheeked doll in a green frock, he placed it in the door of the house, saying, with great pride : "An' this from Griff O'Meara. Heaven bless her swate soul ! "

Just then Nancy Pansy stirred and opened her eyes. Her mother bent over her, and she smiled faintly. Mrs. Seddon slipped down on her knees.

"Where's my old doctor and my dolly ? " she said ; and then, presently, "Where's Harry and Tom Adams ? "

s

"JACK AND JAKE."

I.

"JACK AND JAKE." This is what they used to be called. Their names were always coupled together. Wherever you saw one, you were very apt to see the other—Jack, slender, with yellow hair, big gray eyes, and spirited look; and Jake, thick-set and brown, close to him, like his shadow, with his shining skin and white teeth. They were always in sight somewhere; it might be running about the yard or far down on the plantation, or it might be climbing trees to look into birds' nests—which they were forbidden to trouble—or wading in the creek, riding in the carts or wagons about the fields, or following the furrow, waiting a chance to ride a plough-horse home.

Jake belonged to Jack. He had been given to him by his old master, Jack's grandfather, when Jack was only a few years old, and from that time the two boys were rarely separated, except at night.

Jake was a little larger than Jack, as he was somewhat older, but Jack was the more active. Jake was dull; some

people on the plantation said he did not have good sense ;
but they rarely ventured to say so twice to Jack. Jack said
he had more sense than any man on the place. At least, he
idolized Jack.

At times the people commented on the white boy being
so much with the black ; but Jack's father said it was as
natural for them to run together as for two calves—a black
one and a white one—when they were turned out together ;
that he had played with Uncle Ralph, the butler, when they
were boys, and had taught the latter as much badness as
he had him.

So the two boys grew up together as " Jack and Jake,"
forming a friendship which prevented either of them ever
knowing that Jake was a slave, and brought them up as
friends rather than as master and servant.

If there was any difference, the boys thought it was
rather in favor of Jake ; for Jack had to go to school, and sit
for some hours every morning " saying lessons " to his aunt,
and had to look out (sometimes) for his clothes, while Jake
just lounged around outside the school-room door, and could
do as he pleased, for he was sure to get Jack's suit as soon as
it had become too much worn for Jack.

The games they used to play were surprising. Jack
always knew of some interesting thing they could " make
'tence " (that is, pretence) that they were doing. They
could be fishers and trappers, of course ; for there was the
creek winding down the meadow, in and out among the

heavy willows on its banks; and in the holes under the fences and by the shelving rocks, where the water was blue and deep, there were shining minnows, and even little perch; and they could be lost on rafts, for there was the pond, and with their trousers rolled up to their thighs they could get on planks and pole themselves about.

But the best fun of all was "Injins." Goodness! how much fun there was in Injins! There were bows and arrows, and tomahawks, and wigwams, and fires in the woods, and painted faces, and creeping-ups, and scalpings, and stealing horses, and hot pursuits, and hidings, and captures, and bringing the horses back, and the full revenge and triumph that are dear to boys' hearts. Injins was, of all plays, the best. There was a dear old wonderful fellow named Leatherstocking, who was the greatest "Injin"-hunter in the world. Jack knew all about him. He had a book with him in it, and he read it and told Jake; and so they played Injins whenever they wanted real fun. It was a beautiful place for Injins; the hills rolled, the creeks wound in and out among the willows, and ran through thickets into the little river, and the woods surrounded the plantation on all sides, and stretched across the river to the Mont Air place, so that the boys could cross over and play on the other side of the thick woods.

When the war came, Jack was almost a big boy. He thought he was quite one. He was ten years old, and grew old two years at a time. His father went off with the army,

and left his mother at home to take care of the plantation
and the children. That included Ancy and wee Martha ;
not Jack, of course. So far from leaving any one to take
care of Jack, he left Jack to take care of his mother. The
morning he went away he called Jack to him and had a talk
with him. He told him he wanted him to mind his mother,
and look out for her, to help her and save her trouble, to
take care of her and comfort her, and defend her always like
a man. Jack was standing right in front of him, and when
the talk began he was fidgety, because he was in a great
hurry to go to the stable and ride his father's horse Warrior
to the house ; but his father had never talked to him so
before, and as he proceeded, Jack became grave, and when
his father took his hand, and, looking him quietly in the
eyes, said, " Will you, my son ?" he burst out crying, and
flung his arms around his father's neck, and said, " Yes,
father, I will."

He did not go out of the house any more then ; he left
the horse to be brought down by Uncle Henry, the carriage-
driver, and he sat quietly by his father, and kept his eyes
on him, getting him anything he wanted ; and he waited on
his mother ; and when his father went away, he kissed him,
and said all over again that he would do what he promised.
And when his mother locked herself in her room afterward,
Jack sat on the front porch alone, in his father's chair, and
waited. And when she came out on the porch, with her
eyes red from weeping and her face worn, he did not say

anything, but quietly went and got her a glass of water. His father's talk had aged him.

For the first two years, the war did not make much difference to Jack personally. It made a difference to the country, and to the people, and to his mother, but not to Jack individually, though it made a marked difference in him. It made him older. His father's words never were forgotten. They had sobered him and steadied him. He had seen a good deal of the war. The troop trains passed up the railroad, the soldiers cheering and shouting, filling the cars and crowding on top of them ; the army, or parts of it, marched through the country by the county roads, camping in the woods and fields. Many soldiers stopped at Jack's home, where open house was kept, and everything was gladly given to them. All the visitors now were soldiers. Jack rode the gentlemen's horses to water, with Jake behind him, if there was but one (in which case the horse was apt to get several waterings), or galloping after him, if there were more. They were hard riders, and got many falls, for the young officers were usually well mounted, and their horses were wild. But a fall was no disgrace. Jack remembered that his father once said to him, when a colt had thrown him, "All bold riders get falls ; only those do not who ride tame horses."

All the visitors were in uniform ; all the talk was of war ; all thoughts were of the Confederacy. Every one was enthusiastic. No sacrifices were too great to be made. The

corn-houses were emptied into the great, covered, blue army
wagons; the pick of the horses and mules was given up.
Provisions became scanty and the food plain ; coffee and tea
disappeared ; clothes that were worn out were replaced by
homespun. Jack dressed in the same sort of coarse, grayish
stuff of which Jake's clothes used to be made ; and his boots
were made by Uncle Dick at the quarters ; but this did not
trouble him. It was rather fun than otherwise. Boys like
to rough it. He had come to care little for these things.
He was getting manlier. His mother called him her pro-
tector ; his father, when he came home, as he did once or
twice a year, called him "a man," and introduced him to his
friends as " my son."

His mother began to consult him, to rely on him, to
call on him. He used to go about with her, or go for her
wherever she had business, however far off it might be.

The war had been going on two years, when the enemy
first reached Jack's home. It was a great shock to Jack, for
he had never doubted that the Confederates would keep them
back. There had been a great battle some time before, and
his father had been wounded and taken prisoner (at first he
was reported killed). But for that, Jack said, the "Yankees"
would never have got there. The Union troops did not
trouble Jack personally ; but they made a great deal of
trouble about the place. They took all the horses and
mules that were good for anything and put them in their
wagons. This was a terrible blow to Jack. All his life he

had been brought up with the horses ; each one was his pet
or his friend.

After that the war seemed to be much more about Jack's
home than it had been before. The place was in the possession first of one army and then of the other, and at last, one
winter, the two armies lay not far apart, with Jack's home
just between them. "The Yankees" were the nearer.
Their pickets were actually on the plantation, at the ford,
and at the bridge over the little river into which the creek
emptied, in the big woods. There they lay, with their camps
over behind the hills, a mile or two farther away. At night
the glow of their camp-fires could be seen. Jack had a
pretty aunt who used to stay with his mother, and many
young officers used to come over from the Confederate side
to see her. In such cases, they usually came at night, leaving their horses, for scouting parties used to come in on
them occasionally and stir them up. Once or twice skir-
mishes took place in the fields beyond the creek.

One evening a party of young officers came in and took
supper. They had some great plan. They were quite mysterious, and consulted with Jack's mother, who was greatly
interested in them. They appeared a little shy of talking
before Jack ; but when his mother said he had so much judg-
ment that he could be trusted, they talked openly in his presence. They had a plan to go into the Federal camp that
night and seize the commanding officer. They wanted to
know all the paths. Jack could tell them. He was so

proud. There was not a cow-path he did not know for two
or three miles around, for he and Jake had hunted all over
the country. He could tell them everything, and he did so
with a swelling heart. They laid sheets of paper down on
the dining-table, and he drew them plans of the roads and
hills and big woods ; showed where the river could be waded,
and where the ravines were. He asked his mother to let him
go along with them, but she thought it best for him not
to go.

They set out at bed-time on foot, a half-dozen gay young
fellows, laughing and boasting of what they would do, and
Jack watched them enviously as their forms faded away in the
night. They did not succeed in capturing the officer ; but
they captured a number of horses and a picket at the bridge,
and came off triumphant, with only one or two of their number slightly wounded. Shortly afterwards they came over,
and had a great time telling their experiences. They had
used the map Jack made for them, and had got safely beyond
the pickets and reached the camp. There, finding the sen-
tries on guard, they turned back, and taking the road,
marched down on the picket, as if they had come to relieve
them. Coming from the camp in this way, they had got
upon the picket, when, suddenly drawing their pistols and
poking them up against the Yankees, they forced them to
surrender, and disarmed them. Then taking two of them
off separately, they compelled them to give the countersign.
Having got this, they left the prisoners under guard of two

HE DREW THEM PLANS OF THE ROADS AND HILLS AND BIG WOODS.

of their number, and the rest went back to camp. With the
countersign they passed the sentry, and went into the camp.
Then they found that the commanding officer had gone off
somewhere, and was not in camp that night, and there were
so many men stirring about that they did not dare to wait.
They determined, therefore, to capture some horses and
return. They were looking over the lines of horses to take
their pick when they were discovered. Each man had
selected a horse, and was trying to get him, when the alarm
was given, and they were fired on. They had only time to
cut the halters when the camp began to pour out. Flinging
themselves on the horses' backs, they dashed out under a
fusillade, firing right and left. They took to the road, but it
had been picketed, and they had to dash through the men
who held it under a fire poured into their faces. All had
passed safely except one, whose horse had become unman-
ageable, and had run away, flying the track and taking to the
fields.

He was, they agreed, the finest horse in the lot, and his
rider had had great trouble getting him, and had lingered so
long that he came near being captured. He had finally cut
the halter, and had cut it too short to hold by.

They had great fun laughing at their comrade, and the
figure he cut as his barebacked horse dashed off into the
darkness, with him swinging to the mane. He had shortly
been dragged off of him in the woods, and when he appeared
in camp next day, he looked as if he had been run through a

mill. His eyes were nearly scratched out of his head, and his uniform was torn into shreds.

The young fellow, who still showed the marks of his bruising, took the chaffing good-naturedly, and confessed that he had nearly lost his life trying to hold on to his captive. He had been down into the woods the next day to try and get his horse ; though it was the other side of the little river, and really within the Federal lines. But though he caught sight of him, it was only a glimpse. The animal was much too wild to be caught, and the only thing he received for his pains was a grazing shot from a picket, who had caught sight of him prowling around, and had sent a ball through his cap.

The narration of the capture and escape made Jack wild with excitement. All the next day he was in a state of tremor, and that evening he and Jake spent a long time up in the barn together talking, or rather Jack talking and Jake listening. Jake seemed to be doubtful ; but Jack's enthusiasm carried all before him, and Jake yielded, as he nearly always did.

All that evening after they got back to the house Jack was very quiet. It was the quiet of suppressed excitement. He was thinking.

Next day, after dinner, he and Jake started out. They were very mysterious. Jack carried a rope that they got from the stable, and the old musket that he used in hunting. Jake carried an axe and some corn. They struck out for the creek as if they were going hunting in the big woods, which

they entered ; but at the creek they turned and made for
about opposite where Jack understood his friend had been
thrown by the wild horse that night. They had to avoid the
pickets on the roads, so they stuck to the woods.

At the river the first difficulty presented itself ; the bridge
and ford were picketed. How were they to get across? It
was over their heads in the middle. Jack could swim a little,
but Jake could not swim a stroke. Besides, they did not
wish to get their clothes wet, as that would betray them at
home. Jack thought of a raft, but that would take too long
to make ; so finally they decided to go down the stream and
try to cross on an old tree that had fallen into the water two
or three years before.

The way down was quite painful, for the underbrush
along the banks was very dense, and was matted with bram-
bles and briers, which stuck through their clothes ; added to
which there was a danger of "snakes," as Jake constantly
insisted. But after a slow march they reached the tree. It
lay diagonally across the stream, as it had fallen, its roots on
the bank on their side and the branches not quite reaching
the other bank. This was a disappointment. However,
Jack determined to try, and if it was not too deep beyond
the branches, then Jake could come. Accordingly, he pulled
off his clothes, and carefully tying them up in a bundle, he
equipped himself with a long pole and crawled out on the
log. When he got among the branches, he fastened his
bundle and let himself down. It was a little over his head,

but he let go, and with a few vigorous strokes he reached the other side. The next thing to do was to get Jake over. Jake was still on the far side, and, with his eyes wide open, was declaring, vehemently, "Nor, sir," he "warn gwine to git in that deep water, over his head." He "didn't like water nohow." Jack was in a dilemma. Jake had to be got over, and so had his clothes. They had an axe. They could cut poles if he could get back. There was nothing for it but to try. Accordingly he went up a little way, took a plunge, and, after hard pulling and much splashing and blowing, got back to the tree and climbed up. They were afraid the Yankees might see them if they worked too long on the river, as it was a little cleared up on the hill above, so they went back into the woods and set to work. Jack selected a young pine not too large for them to "tote," and they cut it down, and cut off two poles, which they carried down to the river, and finally, after much trouble, worked along the tree in the water, and got them stretched across from the branch of the fallen log to the other bank. Jake could hardly be persuaded to try it, but Jack offered him all his biscuit (his customary coin with Jake), and promised to help him, and finally Jake was got over, "cooning it"—by which was meant crawling on his hands and knees.

The next thing was to find the horse, for Jack had determined to capture him. This was a difficult thing to effect. In the first place, he might not be there at all, as he might have escaped or have been caught ; and the woods had to be explored with due regard to the existence of the Federal pickets, who were posted at the roads and along the paths. If the pickets caught sight of them they might be shot, or even captured. The latter seemed much the worse fate to Jack, unless, indeed, the Yankees should send them to Johnson's Island, where his father was. In that case, however, what would his mother do? It would not do to be captured. Jack laid out the plan of campaign. They would "beat the woods," going up the stream at a sufficient distance apart, Jake, with the axe and corn, on the inside, and he, with the gun and rope, outside. Thus, if either should be seen, it would be he, and if he came on a soldier, he, having the gun, would capture him. He gave orders that no word was to be spoken. If any track was found notice was to be given by imitating a partridge; if danger appeared, it was to be shown by the cat-bird's call of " Naik, naik." This was the way they used to play " Injins."

They worked their way along for an hour or two without seeing any traces, and Jake, contrary to Jack's command, called out to him :

" Oh, Jack, we ain' gwine fine no horse down heah ; dese woods is too big; he done los'. There's a clearin' right ahead here ; let's go home."

There was a little field just ahead, with one old cabin in it ; a path ran down from it to the bridge. Jack replied in the cat-bird's warning note of " Naik, naik," but Jake was tired of working his way through briers and bushes, and he

9

began to come over toward Jack, still calling to him. Suddenly there was a shout just ahead ; they stopped ; it was repeated.

" Who dat calling ?" asked Jake, in a frightened under-tone.

" Hush ! it's a picket," said Jack, stooping and motioning him back, just as a volume of white smoke with blazes in it seemed to burst out of the woods at the edge of the clearing, and the stillness was broken by the report of half a dozen carbines. Leaves and pieces of bark fell around them, but the bullets flew wide of their mark.

" Run, Jake ! " shouted Jack, as he darted away ; but Jake had not waited for orders ; he had dropped his axe and corn, and was " flying."

Jack soon came up with him, and they dashed along to-gether, thinking that perhaps the picket knew where they had crossed the river, and would try to cut them off.

In their excitement they took a way farther from the river than that by which they had come. The woods were open, and there were small spaces covered with coarse grass on the little streams. As they ran along down a hill approaching one of these, they heard a sound of trampling coming towards them which brought them to a sudden stand-still with their hearts in their mouths. It must be the enemy. They were coming at full gallop. What a crashing they made coming on ! They did not have time to run, and Jack immediately cocked his old musket and resolved at least to fight. Just then there galloped up to him, and almost over him, a magnificent bay horse without saddle or bridle. At sight of Jack he swerved and gave a loud snort of alarm, and then, with his head high in the air, and with his dilated red nostrils and eyes wide with fright, went dashing off into the woods.

II.

"THE horse! the horse! Here he is! here he is!"
shouted Jack, taking out after him as hard as he
could, and calling to Jake to come on. In a minute
or two the horse was far beyond them, and they stopped to
listen and get his direction; and while they were talking,
even the sound of his trampling died away. But they had
found him. They knew he was still there, a wild horse in
the woods.

In their excitement all their fear had vanished as quickly
as it had come. Jake suggested something about being cut
off at the tree, but Jack pooh-poohed it now. He was afire
with excitement. How glad his mother would be! What
would not the soldiers say? "You didn't see him, Jake?"
No, Jake admitted he did not, but he heard him. And Jack
described him—two white feet, one a fore foot and one a
hind foot, a star in his forehead, and a beautiful mane and
tail. Jake suddenly found that he had seen him. They went
back to the little open place in the ravine where the horse
had been. It was a low, damp spot between very high banks,
that a little higher—at a point where the water in rainy
weather, running over a fallen log in the hill-side, had washed

out a deep hole—had become nothing but a gully, with the
banks quite perpendicular and coming together.

The stream was dry now except for a little water in the
hole at the tree. Trees and bushes grew thick upon the
banks to the very edge. Below, where it widened, the banks
became lower, and the little flat piece between them was covered with coarse grass, now cropped quite close. The horse
evidently fed there. Jack sat down and thought. He looked
all over the ground. Then he got up, and walked along the
banks around the hole ; then he came back, and walked up
the gully. Suddenly a light broke over his face.

"I've got it, Jake ; I've got it, Jake. We can trap him.
If we get him in here, we've got him."

Jake was practical. "How you gwine ketch hoss in
trap ?" he asked, his idea of a trap being confined to hare
gums. "'Twill take all de plank in de worl' to make a
hoss-trap. Besides, how you gwine git it heah ? I ain' gwine
tote it."

"Who asked you to ?" asked Jack. "I'm going to trap
him like they do tigers and lions."

"I don' know nuttin' 'bout dem beas'es," said Jake, dis-
dainfully.

"No, you don't," said Jack, with fine scorn ; "but I do."

He examined the banks carefully. His first idea was a
pitfall trap—a covering over the hole. But that would not
do ; it might kill the horse, or at least break a leg. His eye
fell on the tracks up to the water. His face lit up.

" I've got it! I've got it! We'll bait him, and then catch him. Where are the axe and corn you had?"

He turned to Jake. His mind up to that time had been so busy with, first, the flight, and then the horse, that he had not noticed that Jake did not have them.

Jake's countenance fell. " I done los' 'em," he said, guiltily.

Jack looked thunderstruck. " Now you just go and find 'em," he said, hotly.

" I los' 'em when dem Yankees shoot we all. I know I ain' gwine back deah," declared Jake, positively. " I ain' gwine have no Yankee shootin' me 'bout a old hoss."

" Yes, you are," asserted Jack. " I'm going, and you've got to go, too." Jake remained impassive. " Never mind, if you don't go I won't play with you any more, and I won't give you half my biscuit any more."

These were usually potent threats, but they failed now. " I don' keer ef you don' play wid me," said Jake, scornfully. " I don' want play so much nohow ; an' I don' want none you' buscuit.   Dee ain' white like dee use' to be."

Jack changed his key.

" Never mind, that was Aunt Winnie's axe you lost. I'm going to tell her you lost it, and she'll cut you all to pieces. I'm mighty glad I didn't lose it."

This was a view of the case which Jake had not thought of. It was true. The Yankees might not hit him, but if her axe were lost, his mammy was certain to carry out her

accustomed threat of cutting him almost in two. Jake announced that he would go, but first stipulated for the biggest
half of the next biscuit, and that Jack should go before.
They set off back through the woods toward the opening
where they had run on the picket, Jack in the lead, and Jake
a little behind. They had gone about a half mile, when they
heard the sound of some one coming toward them at a rapid
rate.

" Run, Jack ; heah dey come," cried Jake, setting the
example, and taking to his heels, with Jack behind him.
They ran, but were evidently being overtaken, for whoever it
was was galloping right after them as hard as he could tear.

" Hide in the bushes," cried Jack, and flung himself flat
on the ground under a thick bush. Jake did the same. They
were just in time, for the pursuers' were almost on them.
Closer and closer they came, galloping as hard as they could,
crashing through the branches. They must have seen them,
for they came straight down on them. Jake began to cry,
and Jack was trembling, for he felt sure they would be killed ;
there must be a hundred of them. But no, they actually
passed by. Jack found courage to take a peep. He gave a
cry, and sprang to his feet.

" The horse ! it's the horse." Sure enough, it was the
horse they had seen ; all this terrible trampling was nothing
but him in the leaves, galloping back toward the spot from
which they had frightened him. They listened until his
long gallop died out in the distance through the woods.

Jake suggested their going back to look and see if he had
gone to the "little pasture," as they called the place; but
Jack was bent on getting the axe, and the corn with which
they proposed to bait him. His reference to Aunt Winnie's
axe prevailed, and they kept on.

They had some difficulty in finding the place where Jake
had dropped the things, for though they found the clearing,
they had to be very careful how they moved around through
the woods. They could see the picket lounging about, and
could hear them talking distinctly. They were discussing
whether the men they had shot at were just scouts or were
pickets thrown out, and whether they had hit any of them.
One said that they were cavalry, for he had seen the horses;
another said he knew they were infantry, for he had seen the
men. Jack lay down, and crept along close up.

Jack's plan was to set a trap for the horse just at the head
of the ravine, where the banks became very steep and high.
He had read how Indians drove buffalo by frightening them
till they all rushed to one point. He had seen also in a book
of Livingston's travels a plan of capturing animals in Africa.
This plan he chose. He proposed to lay his bait along up to
the gully, and to make a sort of alleyway up which the horse
could go. At the end he would have an opening nearly but
not quite closed by saplings inclined toward each other, and
which would be movable, so that they might interlace. On
either side of this he would have a high barricade. He
believed that the horse would be led by the corn which he

would strew along into the trap, and would squeeze through
the pliant saplings, when he would be caught between the
high banks of the gully, and then if he attempted to get back
through the opening, he would push the saplings together.
He would fix two strong poles so that any attempt to push
through would bring them into position. The horse would
thus be in a trap formed of the high banks and the barricade.
They set to work and cut poles all the evening; but it got
late before they got enough for the barricade, and they had
to go home. Before leaving, however, Jack dragged some of
the poles up, and laid his corn along leading up to the gully
to accustom the horse to the sight of the poles and to going
into the gully among them. They fixed the two poles firmly
at the river crossing from the branch of the tree to the bank,
so that they could get across easily, and then they crossed on
them and came home.

Jack was filled with excitement, and had hard work to
keep from telling his mother and aunt about it, but he did
not.

Jake's fear of his mammy's finding out about the axe kept
him silent.

The next afternoon they went down again, taking more
corn with them, in case the other bait had been eaten. There
were fresh tracks up to the pool, so although they did not
see the horse, they knew he had been there, and they went
to work joyfully and cut more poles. They put them into
position across the ravine, and when it got time to go home

they had up the barricade and had fixed the entrance; but this was the most difficult part, so Jack laid down some more corn along the alley, and they went home.

The next day was Saturday, so they had a good day's work before them, and taking their dinner with them, they started out. Jack's mother asked what he was doing; he said, with a smile, " Setting traps." When they arrived the horse had been there, and they worked like beavers all day, and by dinner-time had got the entrance fixed. It worked beautifully. By pressing in between the two sides they gave way and then sprang together again until they interlaced, and pushing against them from within just pushed them tighter together. They laid their bait down and went home. Monday they visited the trap, but there was no horse in it; the grain was eaten without—he had been there—but inside it was untouched. He had pushed some of the poles so that he could not get in. This was a great disappointment. Jack's motto, however, was, " If at first you don't succeed, try, try again," so they refixed it. The failure had somewhat dampened their ardor.

The next afternoon, however, when they went, there was the entrance closed, and inside, turning about continually, with high head and wide eyes, around the edges of which were angry white rims, was the horse. He was even handsomer than they had thought him. He was a dangerous-looking fellow, rearing and jumping about in his efforts to get out. Jake was wild with excitement. The next thing was to take

JACK MADE A RUNNING NOOSE IN THE ROPE AND TRIED TO THROW IT OVER THE HORSE'S HEAD.

him out and get him home. A lasso would be needed to catch him ; for he looked too dangerous for them to go inside the trap to bridle him. Jack strengthened the entrance by placing a few more poles across it, and then put his corn inside the trap, and hurried home to get a rope and bridle. They were dreadfully afraid that some one might see them, for Jack knew he could not keep the secret now if he met his mother, and he had pictured himself, with Jake behind him, galloping up into the yard, with his horse rearing and plunging, and bringing him up right before his mother, with perhaps a half dozen officers around her. They were back in an hour or so with a good rope and bridle.

Jack made a running noose in the rope, and tried to throw it over the horse's head. He had practised this on stumps and on Jake, playing Injins, until he was right skilful at it ; but getting it over the head of a wild and frightened horse was another thing from putting it over a stump, or even over Jake, and it was a long time before he succeeded. He stood on the bank over the horse, and would throw and throw, and fail ; the horse got furious, and would rear and strike at them with his fore-feet. At last, just as he was thinking that he could not do it, the noose went over the horse's head. Jack pulled it taut.

In a second the other end was wrapped twice around a small tree on the bank ; for Jack knew how to "get a purchase." The horse reared and pulled frightfully, but his pulling only tightened the rope around his neck, and at last he fell back choking, his eyes nearly starting out of his head. This was Jack's opportunity. He had often seen young steers caught and yoked this way, and he had bridled young colts. In a second he was in the pen, and had the bridle on the horse, and in another minute he was out and the rope was loosed. The horse, relieved, bounded to his feet and began to wheel again; but he was not so fierce as before. The bridle on his head was recognized by him as a badge of servitude, and he was quieter. It was now late, and he was too wild to take out yet, so Jack determined to leave him there, and come again next day and get him. The next afternoon Jack and Jake set out again for the little meadow in the woods. Jack was bent on bringing his captive home this time, whatever happened.

He did not go until late, for he had to pass the pickets on the road to the river, and he could do this better about dusk than he could in broad daylight. He had an idea that they might think, as he would come from toward the Yankee camp, that it would be all right; if not, he would make a dash for it. He carried a feed of corn with him to give to the horse for two reasons: the first was that he thought he would need it, and, besides, it would quiet him. They crossed at the old tree, not far from the meadow; they had crossed so often that they had made quite a path now. All the way along Jack was telling Jake how he was going to ride the horse, no matter what he did. Jake was to stand on the ground and hold the rope, so that if the horse flung Jack he would not get loose. They approached the trap with great excitement. They were careful, however, for they did not want to scare him. As they drew near they were pleased to find he had got quiet. They came nearer; he was so quiet that they thought probably he was asleep. So they crept up quite close, Jack in advance, and peeped over the bank into the trap. Jack's heart jumped up into his throat. It was empty! he was gone! Jack could not help a few tears stealing down his cheeks. Yes, he was gone. At first he thought he had escaped, and he could catch him again; but no, an examination of the place showed him that he had been found in the trap by some one, and had been stolen. The barricade was pulled down, and the poles of the entrance were thrown back quite out of the way. Besides, there were men's tracks in the wet place on the edge of the pool. Jack sat down and cried. It was some of those Yankees, he knew. Jake poured out all his eloquence upon the subject. This relieved him.

"If I had my gun I'd go right straight and shoot them," declared Jack.

This valorous resolve set him to thinking. He got up, and went down to the gap. He could see the tracks where the horse was led out. He must have "cut up" a good deal, for the grass outside was very much trampled. Jack could see where he was led or ridden away. The tracks went straight toward the clearing where the picket was. They were quite fresh; he could not very long have been taken.

Jack determined to track him, and find out where he was if possible. They set out through the woods. They could follow the track quite well in most places, but in some spots it was almost lost. In such cases Jack followed the method of woodsmen—he took a circle, and hunted until he found it again. The trail led straight to the clearing. As they drew near, Jake became very nervous, so Jack left him lying under a bush, and he crept up. It was so late now that it was getting quite dusk in the woods, so Jack could creep up close. He got down on his hands and knees. As he came near he could see the men sitting about the little old cabin. They were talking. Their guns were lying against the wall, at some little distance, and their horses were picketed not far off, rather in the shadow, Jack observed. Jack lay down at the edge of the wood and counted them. There were five men and six horses. Yes, one of them must be his horse. He listened to the men. They were talking about horses. He crept a little closer. Yes, they were talking over the finding of his horse. One man thought he knew him, that he was the Colonel's horse that had been stolen that night when so many horses were carried off by the Johnnies; others thought it was a horse some of the negroes had stolen from the plantation across the river from their master, and had hidden. There was the pen and the bridle, and there was the path down to the crossing at the river. Jack's heart beat faster; so they knew the crossing. They were very much divided, but on one thing they all agreed, that anyhow he was a fine animal, worth at least three hundred dollars, and they would have a nice sum from him when they sold him. It was suggested that they should play cards for him, and whichever one should win should have the whole of him. This was agreed to, and they soon arranged themselves and began to play cards in the moonlight.

Jack could now make out his horse standing tied near the cabin on the outside of the others. He could see in the moonlight that he was tied with a rope. He crept back to Jake, and together they went further down into the woods to consult. Jack had a plan which he unfolded to Jake, but Jake was obdurate. "Nor, sah, he warn' gwine 'mong dem Yankees; Yankees ketch him and shoot him. He was gwine home. Mammy'd whup him if he didn'; she mought whup him anyway." Jack pleaded and promised, but it was useless. He explained to Jake that they could ride home quicker than they could walk. It was of no avail. Jake recalled that there was a Yankee picket near the bridge, and that was the only place a horse could cross since the ford was stopped up. Finally Jack had to let Jake go.

He told him not to say anything at home as to where he was, which Jake promised, and Jack helped him across the poles at the tree, and then went back alone to the clearing. He crept up as before. The men were still playing cards, and he could hear them swearing and laughing over their ill or good luck. One of them looked at his watch. The relief would be along in twenty minutes. Jack's heart beat. He

10

had no time to lose. He cut himself a stout switch. He made a little detour, and went around the other side of the clearing, so as to get the horse between him and the men. This put him on the side toward the camp, as the men were on the path which led to the bridge. Without stopping, he crept up to the open space. Then he flung himself on his face, and began to crawl up through the weeds toward the horses, stopping every now and then to listen to the men. As he drew near, one or two of the horses got alarmed and began to twist, and one of them gave a snort of fear. Jack heard the men discussing it, and one of them say he would go and see what was the matter. Jack lay flat in the weeds, and his heart almost stopped with fright as he heard the man coming around the house. He could see him through the weeds, and he had his gun in his hands. He seemed to be coming right to Jack, and he gave himself up as lost. He could hear his heart thumping so, he was sure the man must hear it too. He would have sprung up and cut for the woods if he had had the slightest chance; and as it was, he came near giving himself up, but though the man seemed to be looking right toward him, Jack was fortunately so concealed by the weeds that he did not observe him. He went up to Jack's horse, and examined the rope. "Tain't nothing but this new horse," he called out to his comrades. "He just wanted to see his master. I'll put my saddle on him now, boys. I've got him so certain, and I mean to let him know he's got a master." He changed the saddle and bridle from another horse to that, and then

went back to his comrades, who were all calling to him to
come along, and were accusing him of trying to take up the
time until the relief came, because he was ahead, and did not
want to play more and give them a chance to win the horse
back.

Jack lay still for a minute, and then took a peep at the
men, who were all busily playing. Then he crept up. As
soon as he was out of sight, he sprung to his feet and walked
boldly up to the horse, caught him by the bit, and with a
stroke of his knife cut the rope almost in two close up to his
head. Then he climbed up on him, gathered up the reins,
fixed his feet in the stirrup leathers, bent over, and with a
single stroke cut the rope and turned him toward the bridge.
The horse began to rear and jump. Jack heard the men stop
talking, and one of them say, "That horse is loose;" another
one said, "I'll go and see;" another said, "There's the relief."
Jack looked over his shoulder. There came a half-dozen
men on horses. There was no time to lose. Lifting his
switch above his head, Jack struck the horse a lick with all his
might, and with a bound which nearly threw Jack out of his
seat, he dashed out into the moonlight straight for the road.
"He's loose! there's a man on him!" shouted the men, springing to their feet. Jack leaned forward on his neck and gave
him the switch just as a volley was fired at him. Pop, pop,
pop, pop went the pistols; and the bails flew whistling about
Jack's head; but he was leaning far forward, and was untouched. Under the lash the horse went flying down the
path across the little field.

III.

JACK had often run races on colts, but he had never ridden such a race as that. The wind blew whistling by him ; the leaves of the bushes over the path cut him, hissing as he dashed along. If he could pass the picket where the path struck the road near the bridge, he would be safe. The path was on an incline near the road, and was on a straight line with the bridge, so he had a straight dash for it. The picket was just beyond the fork. Jack had often seen them. There were generally two men on the bridge, and a pole was laid across the railing of the bridge near the other side. But Jack did not think of that now ; he thought only of the men galloping behind him on his track. He could not have stopped the horse if he would, but he had no idea of trying it. He was near the bridge, and his only chance was to dash by the picket. Down the path he went as straight as an arrow, his splendid horse leaping under his light weight—down the path like a bullet through the dusk of the woods. The sleepy picket had heard the firing at the clearing up on the hill, and had got ready to stop whoever it might be. They were standing in the road, with their guns ready. They could not make it out. It was only a single horse coming tearing down toward them.

"Halt, halt!" they called, before Jack was in sight; but it was idle. Down the path the horse came flying—Jack with his feet in the stirrup leathers, his hands wrapped in the bridle reins, his body bent forward on his horse's neck, and clucking his tongue out. In one bound the horse was in the road. "Halt!" Bang! bang! went the guns in his very face. But he was flying. A dozen leaps and he was thundering across the bridge. Jack was conscious only that a dark form stood in the middle, throwing up its arms. It was but a second; he saw it shot out into the water as if struck by a steam-engine. His horse gave one splendid leap, and the next minute he was tearing up the road toward home, through the quiet woods, which gave no sound but that of his rushing stride.

Jack had one moment of supreme delight. His mother had got somewhat anxious about him, and they were all on the front porch when he galloped up into the yard, his beautiful bay now brought down under perfect control, but yet full of life and spirit. As they ran to meet him, Jack sprang from the saddle and presented the horse to his mother.

The next day Jack's mother called him into her room. She took him by the hand. "My son," she said, "I want you to carry the horse back and return him to the Yankee camp."

Jack was aghast. "Why, mamma, he's my horse; that is,

he is yours. I found him and caught him and gave him to you."

His mother explained to him her reasons. She did not think it was right for him to keep the horse obtained in such a way. Jack argued that he had found the horse running wild in their own woods, and did not know his owner. This made no difference : she told him the horse had an owner. He argued that the soldiers took horses, had taken all of theirs, and that their own soldiers—the gentlemen who had come to tea—had been over and taken a lot from the camp. His mother explained to him that that was different. They were all soldiers wearing uniforms, engaged openly in war. What they took was capture : Jack was not a soldier, and was not treated as one. Jack told her how he had been shot at and chased. She was firm. She wished the horse returned, and though Jack wept a little for the joint reason of having to give up the horse and the mortification of restoring it to the Yankees, he obeyed. He had some doubt whether he would not be captured ; but his mother said she would write a letter to the commanding officer over there, explaining why she returned the horse, and this would be safe-conduct. She had known the colonel before the war, and he had once stopped at her house after a little battle beyond them. Colonel Wilson had, in fact, once been a lover of hers.

The idea of going with a safe-conduct was rather soothing to Jack's feelings ; it sounded like a man. So he went and fed the horse. Then he went and asked Jake to go with

him. Jake was very doubtful. He was afraid of the Yankees catching him. The glory of Jack's capture the night
before had, however, given Jack great prestige, and when
Jack told him about the letter his mother was going to write
as a safe-conduct--like a " pass," he explained—Jake agreed
to go, but only on condition that he might carry the pass.
To this Jack consented. It was late in the afternoon when
they started, for the horse had to be broken to carry double,
and he was very lively. Both Jack and Jake went off again
and again. At last, however, they got him steady, and set
out, Jack in the saddle, and Jake behind him clinging on.
Jake had the letter safe in his pocket for their protection.
They had a beautiful ride through the woods, and Jack
remembered the glorious race he had had there the night
before. As they approached the bridge, Jack thought of
tying his handkerchief on a stick as a flag of truce ; but he
was not sure, as he was not a real soldier, he ought to do so.
He therefore rode slowly on. He pictured to himself the
surprise they would have when he rode up, and they recognized the horse, and learned that he had captured it.

This feeling almost did away with the mortification of
having to return it. He rode slowly as he neared the bridge,
for he did not want them to think he was a soldier and shoot
at him. Jack was surprised when he got to the bridge to find
no men there. He rode across, and not caring to keep up
the main road, turned up the path toward the clearing. He
rode cautiously. His horse suddenly shied, and Jack was

startled by some one springing out of the bushes before him
and calling " Halt !" as he flung up his gun. Jake clutched
him, and Jack halted. Several men surrounded them, and
ordered them to get down. They slipped off the horse, and
one of the men took it. They all had guns.

" Why, this is the Colonel's thoroughbred that was stolen
two weeks ago," declared one of the men. " Where did you
steal this horse ?" asked another of them, roughly.

" We did not steal him." asserted Jack, hotly. " We
found him and caught him in the woods."

" You hear that ?" The man turned to his comrades.
" Come, little Johnnie, don't tell lies. We've got you, and
you were riding a stolen horse, and there were several others
stolen at the same time. You'd better tell the truth, and
make a clean breast of it, if you know what's good for you."

Jack indignantly denied that he had stolen the horse, and
told how they had caught him and were bringing him back.
He had a letter from his mother to Colonel Wilson, he
asserted, to prove it.

" Where is the letter ?" they asked

Jack turned to Jake. " Jake's got it in his pocket."

" Yes, I got de pass," declared Jake, feeling in his pocket.
He felt first in one and then another. His countenance fell.
" Hi ! I done los' it," he asserted.

The soldiers laughed. That was a little too thin, they
declared. Come, they must go with them. They proposed
to put a stop to this horse-stealing. It had been going on

long enough. A horse was stolen only last night, and the man had run over one of the pickets on the bridge, and had knocked him into the river and drowned him. They were glad to find who it was, etc.

Jack felt very badly. Jake came close up to him and began to whisper. " Jack, what dey gwine do wid us ? " he asked.

" Hang you, you black little horse-stealing imp ! " said one of the men, with a terrific force. " Cut you up into little pieces."

The others laughed. Men are often not very considerate to children. They do not realize how helpless children feel in their power. Both Jack and Jake turned pale.

Jake was ashy. " Jack, I told you not to come," he cried.

Jack acknowledged the truth of this. He had it on his tongue's end to say, " What did you lose the letter for ? " but he did not. He felt that as his father's son he must be brave. He just walked close to Jake and touched him. " Don't be scared," he whispered. " We will get away."

Just then one of the men caught Jake and twisted his arm a little. Jake gave a little whine of fright. In an instant Jack snatched a gun from a man near by him, and cocking it, levelled it at the soldier. " Let Jake go, or I'll blow your brains out," he said.

A hand seized him from behind, and the gun was jerked out of his hand. It went off, but the bullet flew over their heads. There was no more twisting of Jake's arm, however.

The soldiers, after this, made them march along between them. They carried them to the clearing where the old house was, and where some of their comrades were on guard awaiting them. They marched the boys up to the fire. " We've got the little horse-thieves," they declared. " They were coming over after another horse ; but I guess we'll break it up now."

" Why, they are mighty little fellows to be horse-thieves,'' said one.

" They are the worst kind," declared the other.

" Must be right bad, then, corporal, for you are pretty handy yourself," declared a comrade.

" We are not any horse-thieves," asserted Jack. " We found this horse."

" Shut up !" ordered one of his captors. They began to talk about what they would do with them. Several methods of securing them were proposed, and it was finally determined to lock them up in the loft of the old cabin tili morning, when they would carry them to camp, and the Colonel would make proper disposition of them.

" Can't they get away in there ? " asked one man.

" No ; there is a bolt on the outside of the door," said another. " Besides, we are all down here."

They were accordingly taken and carried into the house and up the rickety old stairs to the loft, where they were left on the bare floor with a single blanket. It was quite dark in there, and Jack felt very low down as he heard the bolt

pushed into the staple on the outside. Jake was crying, and
Jack could not help sobbing a little himself. He had, however, to comfort Jake, so he soon stopped, and applied himself to this work. The only comfort Jake took was in his
assurance that he would get him out.

"How you gwine do it?" asked Jake.

"Never mind, I'll do it," declared Jack, though he had no
idea how he was to make good his word. He had taken
good notice of the outside of the cabin, and now he began
to examine the inside. As his eyes became accustomed to
the darkness, he could see better, and as they were bare-
footed, they could walk about without any noise. The old
roof was full of holes, and they could see the sky grow white
with the rising moon. There was an old window in one end
of the loft. There were holes in the side, and looking out,
Jack could see the men sitting about, and hear their voices.
Jack tried the window; it was nailed down. He examined
it carefully, as he did every other part of the room. He
decided that he could cut the window out in less time than
he could cut a hole through the roof.

He would have tried the bolt, but some of the men were
asleep in the room below, and they could not pass them.
If they could get out of the window, they might climb down
the chimney. He had nothing but his old pocket-knife, and
unfortunately a blade of that was broken; but the other was
good. He told Jake his plan, who did not think much of it.
Jack thought it was bedtime, so he knelt down and said his

prayers. When he prayed for his mother he felt very badly, and a few tears stole out of his eyes. When he was done, Jack began to work. He worked carefully and quietly at first, making a cut or two, and then listening to see if any one stirred below. This was slow work, and after a while he began to cut harder and faster. It showed so very little that he presently got impatient, and dug his knife deeper into the plank. It took a good hold, he gave a vigorous pull, and the blade snapped off in the middle. It made so much noise that one of the men below asked :

"What are those boys doin' upstairs there ? They ain't tryin' to git away, yo' s'pose, are they ? If so, we better fetch 'em down here."

Jack flung himself down beside Jake and held his breath. The soldiers listened, and then one of them said :

"Oh, no, 'tain't nothin' but rats. They're fast asleep, I guess."

Jack almost gave himself up for lost, for he now had only his broken blade ; but after a while he went at it again, more carefully. He could see that he was making headway now, and he kept on cutting. Jake went fast asleep in the blanket, but Jack kept on. After a time he had nearly cut out one of the planks ; he could get a hold on it and feel it give. At this point his impatience overcame him. He took hold and gave a wrench. The plank broke with a noise which startled not only Jake lying in his blanket, but the men below, one or two of whom sprang up. They began to discuss the noise.

" That war'n't no rats," said one. " Them boys is trying to git out. I heard the window open. Go and see what they are doing," he said to his comrade.

Jack held his breath.

" You go yourself," said he. " I say it's rats."

" Rats ! You've got rats," said the other. " I'll go, just to show you 'tain't rats."

He got up, and taking a torch, came to the stair. Jack felt his heart jump up in his mouth. He just had time to stuff his hat into the hole he had made, to shut out the sky, and to fling himself down beside Jake and roll up in the blanket, when the bolt was pulled back and the man entered. He held the torch high above his head and looked around. Jack felt his hair rise. He could hear his heart thumping, and was sure the man heard it too. Jake stirred. Jack clutched him and held him. The man looked at them. The flame flickered and died, the man went out, the bolt grated in the staple, and the man went down the shaky stair.

" Well, you are right for once," Jack heard him say. " Must have been rats ; they are both fast asleep on the floor."

Jack waited till the talk died away, and then he went to work again. He had learned a lesson by this time, and he worked carefully. At last he had the hole big enough to creep through. It was right over the shoulder of the rickety old log chimney, and by making a quick turn he could catch hold of the " chinking " and climb down by it. He could see

the men outside, but the chimney would be partly between
them, and as they climbed down the shadow would, he believed,
conceal them. He did not know how long he had been working, so he thought it best not to wait any longer. Therefore,
after taking a peep through the cracks down on the men
below, and finding them all asleep, he began to wake Jake.
Having got him awake, he lay down by him and whispered
his plans to him. He would go first to test the chimney, and
then Jake would come. They were not to speak under any
circumstances, and if either slipped, they were to lie perfectly
still. The blanket—except one piece, which he cut off and
hung over the hole to hide the sky, in case the men should
come up and look for them—was to be taken along with
them to fling over them if their flight should be discovered.
The soldiers might think it just one of their blankets. After
they got to the woods, they were to make for their tree. If
they were pursued, they were to lie down under bushes and
not speak or move. Having arranged everything, and fastened the piece of blanket so that it hung loosely over the
hole, allowing them to get through, Jack crawled out of the
window and let himself down by his hands. His bare feet
touched the shoulder of the chimney, and letting go, he
climbed carefully down. Jake was already coming out of the
window. Jack thought he heard a noise, and crept around
the house through the weeds to see what it was. It was
only a horse, and he was turning back, when he heard a great
racket and scrambling, and with a tremendous thump Jake

came tumbling down from the chimney into the weeds. He
had the breath all knocked out of him, and lay quite still.
Jack heard some one say, "What on earth was that?" and he
had only time to throw the blanket over Jake and drop down
into the weeds himself, when he heard the man come striding
around the house. He had his gun in his hand. He passed
right by him, between him and the dark blanket lying in the
corner. He stopped and looked all around. He was not ten
feet from him, and was right over the blanket under which Jake
lay. He actually stooped over, as if he was going to pull the
blanket off of Jake, and Jack gave himself up for lost. But
the man passed on, and Jack heard him talking to his comrades about the curious noise. They decided that it must
have been a gun which burst somewhere. Jack's heart
was in his mouth about Jake. He wondered if he was
killed. He was about to crawl up to him, when the blanket stirred and Jake's head peeped out, then went back.
"Jake, oh, Jake, are you dead?" asked Jack, in a whisper.

"I dun know; b'lieve I is," answered Jake. "Mos' dead,
anyway."

"No, you ain't. Is your leg broke?"

"Yes."

"No, 'tain't," encouraged Jack. "Waggle your toe; can
you waggle your toe?"

"Yes; some, little bit," whispered Jake, kicking under
the blanket.

"Waggle your other toe—waggle all your toes," whispered Jack.

The blanket acted as if some one was having a fit under it.

"Your leg ain't broke; you are all right," said Jack. "Come on."

Jake insisted that his leg was broken, and that he could not walk.

"Crawl," said Jack, creeping up to him. "Come on, like Injins. It's getting day." He started off through the weeds, and Jake crawled after him. His ankle was sprained, however, and the briers were thick, and he made slow progress, so Jack crawled along by him through the weeds, helping him.

They were about half way across the little clearing when they heard a noise behind them; lights were moving about in the house, and, looking back, Jack saw men moving around the house, and a man poked his head out of the window.

"Here's where they escaped," they called Another man below the window called out, "Here's their track, where they went. They cannot have gone far. We can catch them." They started toward them. It was the supreme moment.

"Run, Jake; run for the woods," cried Jack, springing to his feet and pulling Jake up. They struck out. Jake was limping, however, and Jack put his arm under him and supported him along. They heard a cry behind them of, "There they go! catch them!" But they were almost at the woods, and a second later they were dashing through the bushes, heading straight for their crossing at the old tree. After a time they had to slow up, for Jake's ankle pained him. Jack carried him on his back; but he was so heavy he had frequently to rest, and it was broad day before they got near the river. They kept on, however, and after a time reached the stream. There Jake declared he could not cross the poles. Jack urged him, and told him he would help him across. He showed him how. Jake was unstrung, and could not try it. He sat down and cried. Jack said he would go home and bring him help. Jake thought this best. Jack crawled over the pole, and was nearly across, when, looking back, he saw a number of soldiers on the hill riding through the woods.

"Come on, Jake; here they come," he called. The soldiers saw him at the same moment, and some of them started down the hill. A shot or two were fired toward them; Jake began to cry. Jack was safe, but he turned and crawled back over the pole toward him. "Come on, Jake; they are coming. They won't hit you—you can get over."

Jake started; Jack waited, and reached out his hand to him. Jake had gotten over the worst part, when his foot slipped, and with a cry he went down into the water. Jack caught his hand, but it slipped out of his grasp. He came up with his arms beating wildly. "Help—help me!" he cried, and went down again. In went Jack head foremost,

11

and caught him by the arm. Jake clutched him. They came
up. Jack thought he had him safe. " I've got you," he said.
" Don't——" But before he could finish the sentence, Jake
flung his arm around his neck and choked him, pulling him
down under the water, and getting it into his throat and nostrils. Jack struggled, and tried to get up, but he could not ;
Jake had him fast. He knew he was drowning. He remembered being down on the bottom of the river and thinking that if he could but get Jake to the top again he would
be safe. He thought that the Yankees might save him. He
tried, but Jake had him tight, choking him. He thought
how he had brought him there ; he thought of his mother
and father, and that he had not seen his mother that morning, and had not said his prayers, and then he did not know
anything more.

The next thing he knew, some one said, " He's all right,"
and he heard confused voices, and was suffering some in his
chest and throat, and he heard his mother's voice, and opening his eyes he was in a tent. She was leaning over him,
crying and kissing him, and there were several gentlemen
around the bed he was on. He was too weak to think much,
but he felt glad that his mother was there. " I went back
after Jake," he said, faintly.

" Yes, you did, like a man," said a gentleman in an officer's uniform, bending over him. " We saw you."

Jack turned from him. " Mother," he said, feebly, " we
carried the horse back, but——"

" He is just outside the door," said the same gentleman ; " he belongs to you.   His owner has presented him to you."

" To me and Jake !" said Jack.   " Where is Jake ?"   But they would not let him talk.   They made him go to sleep.

THE END.

STORIES FOR BOYS.

BY RICHARD HARDING DAVIS.

With Six full-page Illustrations. One volume, 12mo, - - $1.00.

"THE WAVE SWEPT BY HER AND THE DEFEATED CREW SALUTED THE VICTORS WITH CHEERS."

In freshness of theme and originality of treatment, these boys' stories are characteristic of the popular author of "Gallegher," who is himself an expert in all manly sports. Mr. Davis puts an immense amount of snap and dash into these exciting stories of the sports that all wide-awake, healthy boys are interested in, with just a touch of pathos here and there to emphasize some manly trait in his young heroes of the field and the water. Every boy will find them rattling good stories.

TWO BOOKS FOR BOYS AND GIRLS.

Mr. Beard has added sixty new drawings to his "American Boy's Handy Book," to illustrate the new games, sports, and mechanical contrivances which he has incorporated in this latest edition. The Misses Beard's companion volume, "The American Girl's Handy Book," is reduced in price, all the features being retained. Both are profusely illustrated with hundreds of pictures and designs, and in their new dress will be prime favorites with holiday buyers.

THE AMERICAN BOY'S HANDY BOOK:

OR, *WHAT TO DO AND HOW TO DO IT.*

BY DANIEL C. BEARD.

With over 360 Illustrations by the Author.

One volume, square 8vo, - - - $2.00

"The book has this great advantage over its predecessors, that most of the games, tricks, and other amusements described in it are new. It treats of sports adapted to all seasons of the year; it is practical, and it is well illustrated "—*The New York Tribune.*

"It tells boys how to make all kinds of things—boats, traps, toys, puzzles, aquariums, fishing tackle; how to tie knots, splice ropes, to make bird-calls, sleds, blowguns, balloons; how to rear wild birds, to train dogs, and do the thousand and one things that boys take delight in. The book is illustrated in such a way that no mistake can be made."—*The Indianapolis Journal.*

THE AMERICAN GIRL'S HANDY BOOK;

OR, *HOW TO AMUSE YOURSELF AND OTHERS.*

BY LENA AND ADELIA B. BEARD.

With over 500 Illustrations by the Authors.

One volume, square 8vo, - - - $2.00

LOUISA M. ALCOTT WROTE:

"I have put it in my list of good and useful books for young people, as I have many requests for advice from my little friends and their anxious mothers. I am most happy to commend your very ingenious and entertaining book."

GRACE GREENWOOD WROTE:

"It is a treasure which, once possessed, no practical girl would willingly part with. It is an invaluable aid in making a home attractive, comfortable, artistic and refined. The book preaches the gospel of cheerfulness, industry, economy and comfort."

www.ingramcontent.com/pod-product-compliance
Lightning Source LLC
Chambersburg PA
CBHW022359020726

47500CB00002B/360